The Masters Review

ten stories

Best Emerging Writers 2024

To receive new fiction, contest deadlines,
and other curated content right to your inbox,
send an email to newsletter@mastersreview.com

The Masters Review

ten stories

Best Emerging Writers 2024

Jacqueline Gu • Beth Richards

Margaret Adams • Elizabeth Kleinfeld

Aurora Huiza • Emilie Pascale Beck

River Lucero • Jillian Weiss

Vicky Grut • Laura Price Steele

Stories Selected by
Gina Chung

RED MARE
PRESS

Contents

Introduction

I'm often asked what I like to read, or what kind of work pulls me in. This is both a deeply interesting and difficult question (and one that I myself have put to other readers and writers, much to their consternation). While we all inherently know when a particular story makes us sit up in our seats and pay close attention, it's much harder to describe why or how it happens. I sometimes think of it as a quickening of the pulse, or a sensation of recognition—similar to looking across a crowded room into the eyes of someone you love or think you might like to love—ah, there you are, and here I am. In other words, I tend to respond to work that feels, in some way, as if it is speaking back to me. I think this is also why writing is one of the most hopeful things a person can do, since when we set something down on the page, it's generally with the idea that somewhere, someday, someone else might read it too, and understand.

This isn't to say, though, that I read primarily to "feel seen," as people like to say nowadays, or to have my own thoughts and experiences reflected back to me. I'm also looking for imagery, diction, or details that surprise me and make me feel as though something I haven't seen before is occurring on the page. Writing that forces us to slow down, to see anew, and to ask questions of our reality and preconceived notions is just as important as writing that seeks to touch and connect. I think it is here, somewhere between the strange and the familiar, or oscillating across these realms, where we find the best stories, and where the stories in this volume live.

While reading through the shortlist of submissions for this anthology, I found myself thinking a great deal about voice. The way a writer tells a story is informed by specific choices they make along the way, both consciously and unconsciously, and the particularities of that telling—what they choose to notice, remember, and describe—matter just as much as the story itself. The voices represented by these stories are varied and unique, but all of them are insistent and thrillingly alive. In fact, while reading these stories for the first time, I realized that my body usually knew which stories I responded to before my brain did (again: the quickening of a pulse, the straightening of a spine).

While I wasn't reading for any particular themes, I found, in assembling these pieces, that many of them happened to touch on similar ones. These stories ask questions about power, intimacy, control, our imperfect knowledge of one another and the world around us, and the limitations of our frail bodies, as well as the consequences of failing to understand those limitations. There is heartbreak and suffering here, as well as healing, of a kind.

It's my hope that you will read these stories and feel, as I did, both recognized and transported. Perhaps you too will feel your body responding to the ones that you need most.

—Gina Chung
Guest Judge

Fermentation

Jacqueline Gu

The first victim fell ill at a Thai restaurant in Taipei, where he had reportedly eaten a set meal of papaya salad and drunken noodles. Within two hours of the meal, he experienced mild nausea, then fatigue, and then another twenty hours later he was dead. He was a healthy man in his thirties who had recently run a half-marathon, a fact the news broadcasts repeated over and over, airing the same two photos of the man posing with his race medal and dying in the hospital bed side by side. His face was blurred out in both images, lending the collage a kind of threatening vagueness that seemed to say: it could be you, it could be anyone. He was surnamed Zheng, they said. He lived alone and had three cats.

Four more emerged in the following days, all of whom had dined at the restaurant on the same day as Mr. Zheng. Each case followed the same pattern: abdominal pain, vomiting and diarrhea, then rapid organ failure. It wasn't E. coli, or salmonella, or even botulism. None of the usual food poisoning culprits turned up in the bodies of the victims. For days the laboratories tested every ingredient and every contact surface in the restaurant's kitchen for what could be causing the mysterious illness, to no avail, as diners succumbed to renal and liver failure, falling into comas one by one.

Initially, ugly murmurs echoed across the internet, people jumping to point fingers at the Southeast Asian migrant community for so-called unclean food practices. The headlines were blunt and alarmist, emphasizing the ethnicity of the chefs and waitstaff. It's no surprise, Taiwanese locals said amongst themselves, everyone knows their food was dirty to begin with—never mind that it was an upscale restaurant in the lush alleys of Da'an district, frequently patronized by white expats who made six times the average local salary, or that the owner of the restaurant was actually Japanese. But then a new crop of cases emerged, this time from a Taiwanese banquet-style restaurant, where people gathered with their families or coworkers in large groups, or sometimes held weddings. A popular night market was next, specifically one much-beloved stall selling charcoal-roasted pork buns, where at any given time there was a queue snaking down the block. The victims were Taiwanese, German, American, exchange students and white-collar workers and tourists. That put an abrupt end to the accusatory whispers. Online comments laced with overt racism were soon replaced by real panic, as people began to suspect every source of food around them. Anything edible could be tinged with the fatal bacteria, if it was even a bacteria, which no one could confirm.

And in Taiwan, the culture of food was inescapable. There were more restaurants and food institutions per capita in Taipei than in virtually every other metropolitan city in Asia. Many apartments in the city lacked kitchens, including my own; most people I knew who had grown up in Taiwan could not have boiled an egg if held at gunpoint. Everyone worked long hours, after all, and few would choose to go home and cook a balanced meal when there were mom-and-pop shops everywhere, and convenience stores overrun with options for every conceivable food group. But now the entire food chain was potentially tainted. Restaurants began shuttering one by one. Potential danger seeped into the air like spores of mold.

Personally, it was terribly inconvenient timing. My mother was due to arrive in Taipei the following week. It was summer, and being outdoors felt like death by asphyxiation, the heat choking back words as they tried to leave your throat. It was miserably hot, barely habitable in fact, and there was nothing to do besides sit in different air-conditioned rooms to consume various beverages or food. My mother, from the last I remembered, ate as little as she could to survive—but I knew she still wanted to visit night markets and restaurants in her short time here, to experience the culinary landscape of a place she had never been. If the dining options I'd planned to show her all shut down, I had no idea what I would do with her. I felt on edge all week, as if I was walking into an exam I hadn't prepared for.

*   *   *

I had moved to Taipei four years earlier, initially for a teaching position meant to last a year. By the end of it I had fallen in love with a chef at a local bistro who made incredible pasta and talked openly about the breast sizes of the women he had slept with before me. At times he would grab a handful of my belly or my ass and say: this is how everyone knows you're American. He had beautiful hands and a way of looking at me that made me immediately forget the content of everything he had been saying, so all that was left was the melodious tones of a language still new to me. Probably what kept me attached was my failure to understand what he was saying most of the time. That, and his cooking.

Tragically, I had moved to one of the only places in the world with a standard of thinness similar to my mother's. I grew accustomed to the rapid assessments of strangers, who did in fact tell me often that they could tell I was American by the way I carried myself, which I took to mean the way certain parts of my body stuck out more than that of the average Taiwanese woman. My posture worsened, I discovered upon seeing photos of myself, my neck always hunched over slightly, pulled down by the self-consciousness I dragged around with me like an extra limb.

Still, I liked Taipei enough to stay. There was something liberating about slipping under a sea of racial homogeneity, where I was just one anonymous body in a crowd of anonymous bodies. By the time my relationship with the chef ended, I had a new job, a studio apartment all to myself, and a much wider vocabulary for conducting arguments in Mandarin. I had neither the money nor desire to visit my parents back in Illinois, so I hadn't seen them since I'd moved. I felt guilt about this on occasion, like when they sad-reacted to the clipped messages I remembered to send on holidays and birthdays, but it wasn't enough to make me do anything differently. Being away from my old life and all its trappings helped me prune my existence into a shape of my own. Once I had control over my own life, I never wanted to let it go.

*   *   *

The day my mother arrived, I surprised us both by picking her up from the airport. I had never done that before for anyone, yet somehow, I found myself that morning on the subway, feet moving robotically as if I myself were attached to an airport conveyor belt. I suppose the faint aura of crisis that had drifted into the horizon since the illness had emerged was what compelled me to do it, some degree of worry rising out of me in wisps, although I wasn't sure if I was more concerned for her safety or for the inevitable judgments she would pass once she saw what my life here was like. Perhaps being there to intercept her would lend me more control over what she thought. I knew every minute would feel like I had something to prove.

Long before the poisoning incidents broke out, travelers to Taiwan were strictly forbidden from bringing pork products through customs. At the airport there were signs everywhere depicting decapitated cartoon pigs with large red Xs drawn over them, as if to scare you into being a vegetarian. The fine for being caught with pork in any form—which included, for example, a sushi roll containing a single teaspoon of pork floss you had hypothetically bought from your origin airport and forgot to consume on your flight—was up to one million Taiwan dollars. Now, after the outbreak, people traveling to Taiwan were no longer allowed to bring anything consumable at all.

It was an alarming feeling to show up at the airport without any luggage. Surrounded by travelers power walking through security lines, I kept feeling like I had forgotten all my things.

Everyone at the airport was wearing masks again, as if a foodborne bacteria could crawl into one's orifices just from breathing too close to an infected noodle. A group of officers wearing hazmat suits pulled a jar of Marmite out of a sweaty Australian man's bag. People didn't try to avert their stares as he was led into a grim interrogation room.

After making my way to arrivals, I stood awkwardly next to all the people holding up signs with names printed in bold letters, waiting to greet the people they loved. I crossed my conspicuously empty arms and shifted my weight back and forth on my feet. Surrounded by people visibly wearing their emotion, it actually felt inappropriate for me to be there, as if I'd taken a wrong turn and ended up at a stranger's wedding.

People started trickling out of the exit. When my mother came out and saw me, she smiled, then frowned. I felt her eyes roaming over my body and stiffened, hoisting her bag over my shoulder to hide myself from her gaze.

What are you doing here? she said by way of greeting. I had almost forgotten what her voice sounded like. You came all the way out here just to show me how to get to your apartment? I know how to use Google Maps. Don't you have better things to do?

*   *   *

My mother was coming to Taipei not exactly to see me, but rather to use me as a convenient 24-hour layover on her long journey from suburban Illinois to her hometown of Tianjin in China. Her sister was very ill with stomach cancer, which the doctors had only discovered a couple of months before, at which point it had already spread to her liver and lungs. The prognosis was not good. She had remained single her whole life and had no children, so the last person left to take care of her in her final months was my mother. I knew that a substantial part of her didn't want to come at all, to punish her sister for refusing to adhere to societal norms of womanhood and actualize the old threat Chinese women repeated constantly to themselves and their daughters—*if you don't have children, who will take care of you when you're old, you'll die alone.* If there is one thing my mother excels at, even in the face of her only sister's impending mortality, it is the smug finality of *I told you so.*

Still, even though my mother had done what she was instructed and had a child, that child had not made any perceptible effort to see her or speak to her since her sixty-fifth birthday. I wondered if the irony of the situation was lost on her: she who had dutifully done the work of raising a kid but reaped none of the rewards promised by the framework of filial piety, now going to great lengths to act as caretaker for her childless sister, who was supposed to be dying alone.

I didn't want her to acknowledge the strangeness of my going to pick her up from the airport when I hadn't so much as responded to her texts in so many months, because saying it out loud would mean speaking into existence the tensions between us, which had until now existed merely as a vapor that curled around our fingertips. I was fine with things staying that way. I didn't want to kick over the elephant-sized rock to reveal the crawling facts living on its damp underside, such as the fact of my being a cruel and unfilial daughter, because that would then mean having to litigate all the reasons for my being a cruel and unfilial daughter. So when she expressed shock that I was there, I acted like it was a perfectly normal thing for me to be doing. I picked up her bag and headed for the exit, waiting for her to follow.

*   *   *

Our first stop was back to my apartment to drop off her suitcase. I lived just upstairs from a butcher shop, where every day fresh pig carcasses were strung up with twine, partitioned and lined up neatly by body part. It was satisfying to look at, like the inside of a bento box. Usually there were dozens of aunties crowded around the store, clamoring for the butcher's attention in loud tones of dialect, but ever since the outbreak people had been avoiding wet markets.

Now the shop stood empty. But, for some reason, the production of pork had not yet stopped—pigs were still being slaughtered,

I supposed, for meat nobody wanted. My mother gawked at it as we passed by, pausing at the section containing their heads. It had discomfited me when I first moved in to walk by the row of pig's faces hanging overhead, their eye sockets empty and snouts still intact, and I watched as my mother's head swiveled to stare at them as we passed.

That doesn't bother you? she asked me.

Not anymore, I said. Part of me was enjoying this role reversal— my mother, wearing her Sketchers sneakers and North Face windbreaker, looked so vividly American against the backdrop of my neighborhood, where one could see from the peeling paint and faded tiling the sharp traces of how these spaces were passed from generation to generation, so unlike suburban Chicago, where rapid development had flooded neighborhoods with cookie-cutter drywall and saplings so young and frail they reminded one of just-born deer. Now I fit in here, and she didn't. I felt something almost resembling pride.

That was dashed, of course, as soon as I glanced at the expression on her face. She didn't bother to conceal her plain disgust.

You left America? For this? she said in disbelief, as we navigated around potholes on the sidewalk.

The side of my neck was cramping from carrying her bag on my shoulder. I massaged it, exhaling hard, using the sweat on my skin as a lubricant.

The buildings are all old, she said. Everything is falling apart. Wow, that one looks like a dumpster. People live there, seriously?

An elderly man walking beside us glowered at her. The way she spoke Mandarin was louder and brasher than the standard here, the hard *R*s of her mainland Chinese accent ringing like a bell in the street.

I know you don't want to be here, but can you at least try not to talk so loudly? I said. You know everyone here can understand you. People are staring.

Who said I don't want to be here? she said.

My parents had achieved the American Dream at a relatively young age, having moved to the United States for graduate school when they were twenty-two. I wondered, growing up, if they were lonely or homesick or flagged by any of the other descriptors one might expect an immigrant to carry like a loose cape, but for as long as I could remember they'd expressed only enthusiasm for America. They adored Wheel of Fortune and sprawling malls and the idea of the "happy hour." When I told them about my decision to move, the horrified silence over the line was so total that I thought the call had dropped. You're thirty years old and you've decided to be an English teacher in Asia, they said finally, with withering disdain. They probably would have reacted better if I'd told them I'd gotten arrested.

It's possible that I'd only wanted to move to Asia in the first place because I couldn't understand how wholly American they were, and the lack of backstory behind my exterior appearance made me feel disembodied at times, as if I were a video game character to whom my player had given Asian-looking features just for fun.

We entered my apartment and set her things down, and finally her gaze landed on me properly. I felt her eyes dissecting me from head to toe, almost hungrily, seeking out signs of weakness. Instinctively, I stood up straighter, pulling my shoulders back so my collarbones would show.

You've gained weight, she announced, as I knew she would.

Of course, I said dryly. You can always count on me for that.

She, on the other hand, looked more birdlike than I had ever remembered. It was the longest I had gone without seeing her since I moved out at eighteen, and now that she had crossed the border into senior citizenry, every sharp edge previously considered beautiful was exaggerated by the years that had elapsed over the course of her lifetime. Her gray hairs were now white, her thin face sunken, the lines around her mouth etched in permanently by the absence of any fat padding her skin. I wondered how long it had been since she'd eaten a carbohydrate. Her wrist was so slender it actually looked hollow, like a reed.

Well, how much? she asked, unable to help herself. How much do you weigh now?

I stared at her, saying nothing, until the space between us felt waterlogged. I sensed a bare edge of embarrassment in her gaze. Finally she looked away.

*　　*　　*

I had always been a chubby child growing up, to the delight and chagrin of my parents' friends, who could use me as relieved yardstick against their daughters—at least there was always someone bigger than their own. Wow! they would always exclaim upon seeing me. So strong and healthy!

No, she's obese, my parents would say.

It's good to raise someone who's not a picky eater, you don't waste so much, they would always reply, as if my mouth was a garbage chute ready to receive unwanted food at any moment.

Though my parents were deeply Americanized, their foreignness was apparent in ways that included none of the good, such as passing down a language or culinary practice, and only the bad, such as draconian metrics for measuring success and beauty. I had always been aware of my size, and that it was something to be ashamed of, but the distance between my body and a body that would have been deemed acceptable by Chinese standards didn't sink in for me until I got old enough to start caring about clothes.

The first time I went shopping for my own pair of jeans, I was just starting middle school. My mom took me to the mall and led me into stores full of the kinds of shoppers I feared, where huge, blown-up posters of angular white people wearing almost nothing stared down menacingly from the walls. She pulled every size of jeans that could have conceivably fit me off the racks, and in the dressing room, I twisted and mangled my legs in a valiant attempt to squeeze into each pair, to no avail. I could not even fit into the largest sizes. I emerged with my head held low, trying not to look at her or anyone else, wanting very badly to be released. Each successive store was the same: she would hand me armfuls of denim, and I would disappear into the dressing room, alone with the treacherous pants, none of which I could button or even squeeze over my eleven-year-old thighs. I imagined the skin and flesh of my legs as layers of an onion. I fantasized about peeling them off layer by layer and throwing them into the trash.

In retrospect, I suspect my mother did this to me intentionally. She gave me the pants knowing none of them would fit me. She wanted me to feel the hot clasp of shame, she hoped that in that environment, surrounded by girls who were svelte and graceful, like tiny gazelles, I would look myself in the eye and vow to change.

*   *   *

What are we going to eat? she asked me. Is it safe to eat anything?

She looked behind me at the space where there would have been a kitchen if I had one. Instead there was a tiny countertop with a half-eaten bag of potato chips flavored to taste like fried chicken, and two cans of beer. On days I didn't feel like going out to find a real meal, which happened often in the summertime, I would sit on the ground of my apartment in my underwear and mechanically eat from a bag of chips until my stomach hurt, as if I was a subway rat. There was something pleasurable about gorging myself on food so heavily processed it was hardly recognizable as food. When the food poisoning cases broke out, I felt vindicated, like I had actually protected myself by giving into the safety of chemicals processed in a laboratory.

I think we'll have to eat out, I told her. It's not like we can starve.

As if she hasn't already been doing that for the past thirty years, I thought to myself. She frowned and said nothing.

I could see that her curiosity about the cuisine here was at war with herself. If it wasn't for the new laws against importing food, she would have brought protein bars to tide herself over for these two days, but now there was no way around it.

There have only been a few dozen cases so far, I said. Two million people live in Taipei and most of them eat out multiple times a day. The odds are pretty low.

Fine, she said. Let's see what all the fuss is about Taiwanese food anyway.

I took her to a small neighborhood spot that sold traditional breakfast food: hot soymilk, salty dough fritters, rolled egg pancakes.

It was cheap, greasy food served under fluorescent lights, with oil stains dotting walls that looked like they had only ever been cleaned as an afterthought. An old-school antenna TV was affixed to a corner of the ceiling, airing the local news.

I watched her face closely as she dipped the fried dough in the soymilk and took a bite. When she looked disappointed, my heart sank a little in parallel. This is it? she said. It tastes the same as what you get frozen from the grocery store.

It's not that complex of a food, I said. What were you expecting?

I thought Taiwanese breakfast was supposed to be famous, she said.

I took a bite. She was right: the dough fritter tasted stale, like it had been sitting out for a day. I thought of the heat outside and what might happen to food exposed to it for more than a few minutes, shuddering internally. Mmm, I said with relish, not willing to admit defeat.

The news anchor interrupted us with the latest update on the outbreak. All the ambient conversation in the air dissolved. Another fifteen people had fallen ill since yesterday, she said. Nine more had died. For the first time, the new cases detected in a single day couldn't be traced back to just one location, which meant that the illness was beginning to spread faster. It was encroaching.

The owner of the restaurant hastily shut the TV off. The ensuing silence was far louder, as we all tried to pretend we hadn't been clinging to every word of the broadcast. There was no air-conditioning in this restaurant, only a fan whirring overhead, and the sound of the fan expanded into the small space, filling every corner of the room. I felt sweat dripping down my temple. A fruit fly zoomed around my cup of soymilk in figure eights. Out of the corner of my eye I saw a young couple quickly stand up to leave, their food barely touched, steam still rising from the plates.

You left America? my mother said to me again, a quiet hiss. For this?

*   *   *

Not everyone who fell ill died, at least not immediately, although a shockingly high proportion of them did. Twenty-four out of the 113 cases detected thus far were still living, and they appeared on news broadcasts day after day, their faces gaunt, looking almost translucent.

It's awful, really awful, one man said. I can't keep anything down. Every time I think it's over, I keep expelling more.

I really thought I would die, a woman said. I didn't know you could survive from something like that.

The symptoms were always the same at first, identical to any other foodborne illness: nausea, vomiting, diarrhea. It drained the color from their lips, their cheeks, it crept along their veins deeper and deeper into the body. Then, if they were unlucky, it would wrap around the tender motor of their heart and abruptly cut off the blood supply from their organs. They would fall comatose and die, usually within a couple of days.

Many of the survivors on TV looked like they were barely clinging to life. Their visible malnourishment pockmarked the inside of my brain. It was difficult to look away. The little calculators inside my head whirred away with the dull regularity of a white noise machine. I was powerless to stop it. I could probably encircle her entire upper arm with my thumb and middle finger, I thought. Her entire waist could probably fit into my pant leg.

During the worst bout of food poisoning I ever had, I lost enough weight to fit into an aspirational dress my mother had bought for me when I was still a teenager. I was never even close to the right size to wear it, and she dangled it in front of me cruelly, a carrot stick to a donkey. I was in college then and still carried that dress around with me like a cursed rabbit's foot, deciding to hold onto it over and over again at the end of every year as I moved from dorm to dorm. Its evil light gripped me through the years. I was in its power.

When the food poisoning struck me, I spent two weeks throwing up, shitting my guts out, weak with fever and dehydration. Yet every morning my routine was still the same: I would drag myself to the bathroom, remove all my clothes, and step on the scale. At some point I realized that it was a number I had not seen since I was many years younger. And then I remembered the dress. I dug it up from my closet and sucked in. The zipper zipped. I was dizzy with disbelief. It felt as if my body was no longer mine, it no longer belonged to me, it was freed.

I gained it all back, of course, after the virus left me. After that, every time I got sick, a small and treacherous thrill lit up inside me. The vicious thing about illness for people like me: it invites you into the heady illusion of another kind of life, and then, just as rapidly, it yanks it away. With a jolt of whiplash you return to who you always were.

*   *   *

On my phone, I got a notification from the local news channel: authorities had found the cause at last. A particular compound in the rice at that first Thai restaurant, left in specific and unyielding conditions, had fermented, incubating a lethal bacteria. Once it lodged into the bodies of the first victims, it had begun to spread through the various bodily fluids they'd expelled over the course of their illness. It could stay alive in the sewage systems, in the city's water supply, looping all the way back to the manufacturing of other consumable products. In the article, they called it *rice poison*.

We had left the breakfast shop and were sitting down at a teahouse now, drinking hojicha and nibbling on peanut brittle. It looked like everyone got the notification, or some variant of it, at the same time. Don't worry! the owner of the teahouse said cheerily to the room. We use ultra filtered water from mountain springs! Very safe! A nervous-looking woman sitting beside us reached over to pour herself a glass of the reportedly safe water, knocking over a cup of tea. The boss rushed over to clean it up.

My mother seemed unbothered. She took another sip with great satisfaction. She loved tea, parroting articles that claimed caffeine would boost your metabolic rate, and she could name the health benefits and antioxidant value of each tea variety. Our cabinet was full of green tea weight loss supplements that she took religiously. I tried one once, and it made my heart beat like a rabbit's.

Once, when I was in elementary school, I went into the kitchen late at night to get a glass of water. I saw her then, standing at the stove, looking motionlessly at the pot of cabbage soup she was preparing for the next day, or maybe staring at the wall behind it. She hadn't eaten dinner with us in a week, instead replacing each meal with a soup of boiled cabbage that she prepared in batches and microwaved one bowl at a time. A wooden spoon dangled from her hand. She looked so tiny there, not moving even as the pot began to hiss. A small seed of grief bloomed inside me, although I couldn't name it then, slowly unfurling its petals. I watched her from the darkness of the hallway for a minute until the soup boiled over, and then, without making a sound, I went back to my room and shut the door.

*   *   *

I had grown into existence inside her, like a parasite. I emerged from her body. Her body beget mine, she created me, she owned me. I grew and I grew into a meaty, alien thing. For years she must have watched in simple horror.

Everything that came later, everything she did to me, was only her way of trying to help me, I tried to tell myself. She was not equipped to speak to me in anything other than the language of shame.

*   *   *

We left the teahouse to go for a walk in Da'an Park. The sky was overcast, humidity hanging in the air like a wet blanket. It felt somehow wholesome to be sweating so much, as if my insides were being washed. My mother complained that it was too hot and found a bench for us to sit.

On the path in front of us, a jogger paused to drink from his bottle. His face looked grey in the dimming light. And then I heard it: loud retching, impossibly violent. He was bent over in two like a hairpin, then fell down to his hands and knees, vomiting uncontrollably on the road.

Everyone around us scattered in an audible panic. A short distance away, people started taking out their phones to film. I realized we were the last people within a twenty-foot radius of him. I stood to leave, but my mother stayed seated.

What are you doing? I said. We should go.

She was frozen on the bench, staring vacantly at him. An unidentifiable mixture of emotions passed across her face.

We need to leave, I said. You do what you want, but I'm going.

How can you say that? Her voice was suddenly taut. She stood up and gripped my arm with unexpected force. I yanked it back like it had been burned, and she let go. The jogger had reached the stage of retching at which nothing was coming back out. I was no longer facing him, but I could identify it purely by sound.

I started walking. My mother trailed behind me in silence. Just before we exited the park, I turned back to glance at him again. Under the jagged leaves of the breadfruit trees, his silhouette cast a shadow like a memory.

* * *

We left the park to go home, rattled. An alien quiet had descended in the alley by my apartment. A woman carrying several large takeout bags from McDonald's rushed past us, the smell of French fries wafting behind her like a trail of perfume, and scurried into the convenience store around the corner to dump her untouched food in the trash. An elderly man emerged from his restaurant storefront and locked the front door. Though it was only afternoon, I heard the sound of metal grates signifying stores arriving at the end of their business hours slamming up and down the block, echoing bleakly.

Back in my apartment, we watched the news with trepidation. A new early symptom had emerged, a slight yellowing of the skin on one's hands. They showed several examples: the yellows ranged in shade from virtually invisible to the human eye to a hue of neon highlighter. I turned my head to look at my mother. She was leaning against my futon, head tilted down, examining the backs of her hands.

How is your sister doing? I asked her.

She's… well, you know, she said. She's not good.

I looked down at my own hands, which were fidgeting with the trim on a cushion I was strangling unconsciously, and waited for her to continue.

It's such a shame, she said. I always told her she needed to stop eating such heavy foods. She used to add vinegar to everything, even plain cabbage.

What does that have to do with anything? I said.

They're saying the cancer is related to her diet. I always knew it would make her sick. I played with my left earring, clicking it open and closed. I didn't know what to say. You know we were born during the famine, she said. When we were younger, we had nothing. We were always getting sick.

I did know. I had heard the stories of what it had been like for them to grow up during the Cultural Revolution, through the long shadow cast by the Great Famine: the fleshy insects baked inside the plain steamed buns they got at school, the taste of eggs once a year. They'd had an uncle who died in the famine, and their family, being too poor to afford a proper burial, had to leave his bloated body in the field.

It's such a shame, what happened in the end, she said again. I tried to help her, I really did.

After it was all over, my mother and her sister's relationships to food and its scarcity shot off in diametrically opposite directions. As China's economy exploded through the following decades, so too did its food scene, new storefronts springing up with decadent cakes layered like impressionist paintings, oily hot pot crowded with buttery wagyu. My aunt, upon facing this sudden glut of edible luxury, grew to rely on food as her primary source of comfort. Once she learned to eat for pleasure, she couldn't seem to stop. This stomach cancer was like a perverse joke from God.

My mother, on the other hand, learned to exist in the razor-thin boundary between excess and emptiness. She hoarded food, keeping cans of fried dace in the pantry for as many years as I was alive, refusing to let any of us clean out the refrigerator.

Once, digging around for a popsicle that had fallen to the bottom of the freezer, I fished out a plastic bag of unidentifiable meat that had been labeled in her handwriting with the year 2000. She read American cookbooks and baked loaf after loaf of bread, calling me to the kitchen to feed me a fat slice, pouting if I only ate one. The thinner she got, the more she seemed to feast on the act of feeding everyone around her, as if it was enough to project onto us the fantasy of everything she denied herself.

It was my mother who had shown me how to vomit after eating. The first time came on my thirteenth birthday, after we ate at a sushi buffet restaurant. She had taught us to fast for 24 hours before all-you-can-eat meals, like camels storing up their thirst for the first sign of water. When we got back home I laid down in my room, swollen with rice and self-loathing, and she came in and led me to the bathroom. This is how I do it, she told me, demonstrating. In later years, when my esophageal damage was beginning to show, she gifted me boxes of laxative tea, telling me cryptically that it would help me feel cleaner. The text on the packaging was in Chinese, which I could not read. The first time I drank it, I had no idea what was going to happen, or the awareness that anything would happen at all. Twelve hours later, I was on the toilet, stomach writhing in path, releasing what felt like years of accumulated gunk from my intestines. I emerged several pounds lighter, feeling almost holy, having shed excess weight I hadn't realized was sitting in my body. I understood then, with fearsome clarity: this hunger for cleanness must have been stored somewhere in my genetic code. It was an assault of synapses firing across the brain with an urgency I never chose.

After I left home at eighteen, I stopped calling, stopped opening the emails with forwarded links, eventually stopped responding to her WeChat messages. I hadn't engaged in these behaviors in years, but now, seeing my mother again, I felt the old itch. The compulsion to erode oneself must have had its roots in the yearning to belong.

She didn't elaborate more on the status of her sister. She was watching the TV in silence, which was now showing the emaciated bodies of patients in the ICU. I could see the outline of something coagulating behind the fear in her eyes. If I had to describe it, I would say it looked almost like longing.

*   *   *

It was nighttime, and we hadn't eaten all day aside from the few bites of breakfast many hours earlier. A wide ache of hunger was bubbling in my stomach.

Were there any other restaurants you were planning to take me? she asked. Before all this happened.

There were a few, I said. A beef noodle shop, a stir-fry restaurant. A place that serves a bunch of deep-fried stuff you can pick out from a display in front.

She was quiet for a moment. What if we go to the fried stuff shop? Would they still be open?

I glanced at her warily. Really? I said.

Well, it's like you said, she said. Just a few dozen cases, nothing too bad.

I was silent. I thought of the expression on her face when she was watching the victims on the news, how she almost seemed to come alive.

She cleared her throat.

I'll never be here again, she said. I'd like to do this with you.

Her words seemed to slow down, stretch out like taffy. I pinched the skin on my knees and tried to piece together what she was saying.

She looked so childlike on my futon, sitting with her knees up. I imagined her at age nine, going to school with her sister, eating the mantous studded with black flies, and felt lightheaded, like I could disappear. Danger was all around us, it was so mundane, it was almost a miracle we were sitting together in that moment.

Okay, I said finally. Let's go. We walked to the restaurant. It felt like a furnace inside: no air-conditioning, only the potent fumes of frying oil rolling out from the kitchen. The boss was about to close up for the night, and until further notice, but he allowed us to sit when I told him my mother was about to leave town.

He emerged soon with a plate of assorted fried food—juicy pieces of chicken thigh, sticky rice mixed with pork blood and cut into Lego-shaped blocks, enoki mushrooms splayed out in crisp golden fans. The whole assortment was showered in an addictive mixture of MSG, white pepper, and salt. The smell was so rich, so unctuous. I couldn't imagine it hurting us, this luscious pile of food, even though deep down I knew that it could and it would.

I watched as she took a bite. She closed her eyes with obvious pleasure, lips curled almost in a grimace.

We were the only diners left. Condiments sat on the tables of the empty shop, unused, salt crystals clinging to the tips of soy sauce bottles. The tables were a bright plastic red, which cast a burning flush over the walls and tableware. She chewed slowly, with great relish, a slick of oil appearing around her lips.

Thank you for taking me here, she said, so softly I almost couldn't hear. The hollows of her cheeks looked deeper in the red light, her face glowing like a dying ember.

I opened my mouth to say something and felt it dissolve in the back of my throat, a tiny gasp of negative space. There was something ghostly forming around her, something like the hazy shape of desire, or perhaps the silhouette of the body she would have inhabited had she allowed herself to. I wanted to reach out and grasp it. I wanted to hug her body to mine. The moment passed. She took another bite, and it evaporated into the air between us.

JACQUELINE GU is a writer and journalist currently based in Taipei, Taiwan, formerly based in New York. This is her first published fiction.

In Praise of the Collective Noun

Beth Richards

I hear—more than feel—my body hit the wall. The hand that belongs to my mother's husband grips the back of my neck and propels me into the painted sheetrock. He takes a firmer grip. Face and wall collide. I am thirteen, and a third his size. I want to raise my hands, to put them between him and me, or between me and the wall, but they fall uselessly at my side. He grabs my left wrist, twists it behind me. I hear—more than feel—one part of my shoulder tear away from the other, though the blinding flash of light tells me that, somewhere, I hurt.

A noun names a person, place, thing, or idea. I am a thing.

The flash of light behind my eyes is stark, white, like the summer heat outside the window. Over his breathing, the grunt of his effort, I hear singing, a mockingbird. The neighbor's lawnmower putts up and down the boundary between our back yards. I hear myself whimper, not because I feel pain but because I cannot see his face, and I do not know when, this time, he will stop. If he will stop.

My mother stands in the doorway to the room. Her hand is on her hip. I reach toward her with my right hand, wanting her to touch me, to touch him, to stop this. I think she draws away. I know that my nails scrape the hard wood of the doorframe. Her voice, cold, slides in from somewhere, miles away from either of us.

"Hit her again."

He does.

A noun names an idea. One idea: That my mother will protect me from the rage of this man she has married. An idea is still a noun, even if it is not true.

A noun names a person. The pain that remains in my shoulder seems to have a life of its own. I name it "Fred."

A noun names a place. High school is a noun. It is a place where I can sleep and be safe for a while. Church is a noun. It is a place where my mother and sister and I sit—without her husband—and pretend that nothing is wrong in the house where we all live, like trapped animals, together.

Except.

One night, one of the girls in Wednesday night Bible study accidentally bumps my shoulder. My knees buckle but I hold my breath and will myself impervious. I am fourteen now; Fred and I know this routine. I take a deep breath. I tell the girl I am fine.

Behind the girl is her mother, who touches her hand to the small of my back and says, "I just need to see about you" in a voice of such gentleness that I cannot stop myself from moving toward her. She guides me into the restroom, where I watch her face change from pink to gray to white as she peers around my collar, lifts my blouse and then my skirt. With each motion she says, "I'm so sorry. I won't hurt you." I know what she sees on my arms and legs: new, livid purple and blue welts; faded yellow and brown and greenish stripes; round bruises on the back of my neck, the size and shape of fingers.

She touches my left arm; I try to pull away then stop, drop my chin onto my chest, mouth open, to quell the wave of nausea. She places wet paper towels on my forehead and the back of my neck.

"How would you like to spend the night at my house?"

A noun names a place. House is a noun. A house is where people live. A house is where people get hurt. I shake my head.

My mother will never agree. Our business is our business. Her husband will be livid. He... no.

"No."

I wonder what this woman's house looks like.

I remember her hands, where her palms touch my skin feels cool. I am sure I shake my head, *no no no*. The hell there will be to pay if my mother finds out. A hotter hell if she tells her husband. How long are we there in the small bathroom? Probably only a few minutes, but it feels longer as I lean, cow-dumb, into to her tenderness.

We leave the bathroom. My mother is nowhere to be seen. I follow the woman and her daughter to their car, and I spend the night at their house. I have no idea what she says to my mother. The next morning, the woman and her husband ask if I would like to live with them. A different place. With different persons. Where I might not be a thing.

"Yes," I say. "I do."

*   *   *

I am five when I begin first grade. I love book time, where I am the fastest reader, and hate recess, where I am the playground's slowest and smallest, the target of the class bully. In second grade, my high-school-age neighbor sits next to me on the school bus and coaches me on how to defend myself. To repay her, I read her biology textbook aloud to her on the long ride into town. In social studies, I am mesmerized by geography, by the coded lines and symbols on maps. I imagine myself a bird—regal hawk? sturdy robin?—swooping over a bird's-eye view of the landscape, riding invisible currents, first over mysterious land, then over limitless sea.

As my teacher's agitation grows, I add but refuse to subtract. I do not understand the removal as symbolic and thus fear that the thing in question—apples, oranges, cookies, boys, girls—will disappear if I "take away" as ordered. My teacher is relieved when I finally, after weeks of resistance, take eight away from twelve and write the four, clear and sharp cornered, below the line. Though she warns my mother and father—he is still alive then—that I "might not" be very bright.

After school, as I perch in the pecan tree just east of our house, I explore the landscape of language, the adding and subtracting of words and phrases. I don't read—I gobble, slurp, gulp. I dive headlong into whatever book I can get my hands on. Every Beverly Cleary dog-and-girl adventure. *Harriet the Spy*, Pippi Longstocking, Louisa May Alcott, and the entire Little House series. Collections of sing-song poetry. The red-lettered King James Bible that my grandparents gave me when I learned to read. Science books on dinosaurs, trees, horses, and reptiles. On the bus, I steadily make my way through my neighbor's biology textbook, complete with intriguing diagrams of body parts *below* the waist, the region my grandmother refers to mysteriously as "down there."

My grandparents refer to my elementary school as "grammar school," a label I've always thought funny because I have no recall of learning grammar, the systems and structures of language. But because I read so much, I begin to absorb its DNA, the rules for making new word-life—inflection, syntax, word forms—even though I am not yet conscious of grammar as the means to combine all those words in all those ways to make story and sermon, saga and snake tale.

*   *   *

After we begin living with my mother's new husband, after my father dies, I learn some new nouns: weed, speed, liquor, barbs, hash, Camel. I'm sure my English class studies grammar, but I don't remember—not because my teachers are ineffective but because I am, as they say, impaired. Routine can be an adjective, but for me it is a noun: speed in the morning to lever myself out of bed, barbs at night to undo the speed and sag into a few hours of sleep. Creative combinations of alcohol and weed spackle the spaces in between. They allow me to tell people—and perhaps myself—that I am fine. They make the bruises hurt less. They help me forget, at least until the next time, the look on my mother's face, as she looks away. My friend Jodi shows me how to carefully remove tobacco from a Camel and replace the tobacco with hash. A Camelash? A Hashamel? I hate the taste, whatever we call them, and cough until my eyes and nose stream. But they let me forget some other nouns for a while: Fred. Fear.

*   *   *

The woman who decodes the person-thing-idea of my body that night in the church restroom becomes my legal guardian. After the court hearing, my sister places her hands, palms down, squarely against my chest and shoves me as hard as she can. She says she hates me, never wants to see or speak to me again; I have shamed and betrayed us, talking about our business to outsiders. She neatly sidesteps the fact that she moved out of the house before I did—and talked plenty about why.

After the hearing, my mother calls me once, spits into the phone that I have ruined her marriage and destroyed her family. I don't believe her, but I still feel guilty.

*   *   *

In a sentence, a noun can function as subject or object. Subject: a noun that performs an action or is described. Object: a noun that follows or receives the action of the verb or identifies the result of the action.

The man strikes the girl. Object.

The girl picks herself up, walks into a new life. Subject.

*   *   *

When my guardians ask me if I have used drugs or alcohol, I say, "Some." A pronoun. A word that substitutes for a noun. In this case, an indefinite pronoun, which allows me to answer and not answer, at the same time. I don't want to lie, but I am afraid that the definite truth will make them send me away.

And it is the truth, to a point. At my mother's house, I take the drugs to function, to calm Fred, to sleep, to feel like a subject in control of the syntax of my life, not just the object receiving someone else's actions. Unlike my classmates who play pharmaceutical roulette to find the edgiest high, I derive no wild pleasure from my substances. I welcome the energy uptick from the small, white tabs of speed, the sense that if I get upright and in motion, I can figure out a way to navigate the day. I shudder at the taste of liquor, hold my breath while sipping cheap, yeasty beer from a bottle snugged in a brown bag. They don't make the pain go away. They do warm the icy spot that takes up so much space in my chest. At night, as I slide down the dark cliff toward sleep, I know that, for a short time at least, I will be free from feeling anything at all.

*   *   *

My new family applauds my new life as subject—clean and sober, in charge, neatly picking up the new person in a new place. Rebirth. Do we have any idea what we are getting into? None. Both a pronoun (not one) and an adverb (in no way, not at all). The shakes and the sweats, the endlessly itchy skin, and the "dreams" of a room crawling with spiders are (I know now) symptoms of do-it-yourself drug and alcohol withdrawal. During those first nights, as the rest of my new family sleeps, I sweat, shiver, and pace. My shoulder crackles and throbs. I scratch the spiders off my arms and when I am ready to scream, I put a pillow over my mouth and count to ten, to twenty, to one hundred. Addition, not subtraction. I wonder if saying "yes" to a new life as subject is really such a great idea. As object, life had a familiar rhythm that was perversely comforting. In this new life, people look me in the eye and ask me how I feel. I am expected to show up at the dinner table and converse. Each day seems to last three and each night stretches into eternity. And what then? What person, place, or thing lies beyond? While everyone else sleeps I stand at the window, watching the moon wax into full and cross the night sky.

One night about three weeks after I move in, I feel suddenly boneless, so exhausted I can barely climb into bed. I sleep deeply and without dreams. I wake as the sun is rising. I shower, pull on a t-shirt. It slides over my skin, tweaking the scabs on my arms. I look in the mirror, see a cascade of curly hair, deep under-eye circles, a pale, taut face. A person—me. A place—a new home. An idea—I might be safe here. A thing—family? I go downstairs.

My stomach growls so loudly that I stop still, waiting for someone to thunder "Who the hell is making all that noise?" My new parents don't say that. They say, "Are you hungry?" My stomach roars yes before I can reply. They smile, fill my plate with soft scrambled eggs and toast.

*   *   *

A collective noun is a singular form that denotes a group. Examples: team, crowd, jury, audience, family, class, flock. The team plays, using its collective strength, which is mightier than its individual talents. The museum crowd moves from exhibit to exhibit. The jury decides that a mother is no mother after all. The audience gasps at the same time, riding along on the communal emotion that ripples and surges between couples, rows, sections, that sometimes does not fade until long after the movie is over. The family quietly includes a girl in its life, gives her chores, clean clothes, warm food, and a hug at bedtime. The class looks at the new girl in curious anticipation. The flock of blackbirds kiting by her window rises and falls, turns in midair, as if each bird is attached to its multitude of neighbors by a small, exquisitely tuned string, as if they all are one.

Abstract nouns refer to concepts; concrete nouns refer to things perceived by the senses. My new school about a mile from my guardian's house is concrete, literally, with that bland institutional flooring shared by schools, hospitals, and prisons. A bell clangs. The concrete and tile hallways surge with students, who stomp and yell and then miraculously disappear through narrow doorways just as another bell rings. I try to count them then stop, my head spinning. Many wear faded jeans and t-shirts. Some of the girls sport short, tight skirts sandwiched between tall leather boots and frilly, scoop-neck tops. A few are swallowed by oversize football jerseys. A lone male student centers his wide striped necktie over his button-down shirt. I notice that no one speaks to him as everyone clatters through the halls.

More concepts: awkwardness. Loneliness. I am the new kid entering a new school in the middle of the term. All those people move in small, connected groups through the hallways, but I know no one and no one knows me. Collective, minus one. Two, if you count the kid in the tie. Alliances and partnerships have been established well before I arrive. Everywhere I go I feel as if hundreds of eyes are following me. One new girl, both concept and count.

I try to decipher the hierarchy of the student body as they flow by, to see where I might fit in: thick-necked guy stuffed into an Izod shirt: jock. By his side, a pale blonde girl admiring both the guy and her glittering nails: cheerleader. Gaggle of beret-topped kids hollering "Mais OUI!": French Club. I wonder if they can read me as well: "Ward of the court." "Girl whose mother won't protect her." Or maybe just "Trouble."

My assigned guidance counselor clearly falls into the latter category. I wait while he reads my file. He wrinkles his nose. He sighs. I know what he sees: uneven grades, many absences. He "sincerely hopes" I will not cause any trouble in *his* school (possessive pronoun: belonging to him, not me). He is certain that I will "make *better* choices this time" (adjective: of superior quality; more virtuous, obviously not me). He seems to be waiting for me to say something. When I do not, he slaps the file on his desk, says, "Well then, come along," and escorts me to my second-period class.

*   *   *

A noun is a place. All the other students have snagged seats close to the back of the room. I get a front-row seat, all to myself. What I perceive with my senses: I see the orange ball of early-winter sun suspended outside the window. I feel chilled and exhausted. I hear my heartbeat pound in my ears. I taste my dry lips, giving silent thanks that I did not eat the breakfast my guardian offered earlier that morning.

"You need your strength," she said.

I need a drink, I thought, though I didn't say it out loud, given that I was officially clean and sober.

The classroom windows are closed but I can smell the cigarette smoke from the designated smoking area; every cell in my body shifts in its direction. I pull my sweater down over my hands; my arms still feature scratches and scabs in various stages of healing.

Maybe I can cover up the rest of me and hide. Maybe, if I stay very still, no one will notice me.

Common nouns refer to any member of a category. Class. Teacher. Proper nouns are specific names. In this case, English, and Mrs. Kelly. And she is quite specific: five feet tall; shaped like a well-fed pear; thick black hair rounded at the top, a flip at the shoulder-length ends, and a Cruella de Vil streak of white highlighting the crown. A gauzy scarf twines around her neck and flows down her back. Mrs. Kelly strides toward me on brisk, sensible heels, and it takes everything I have not to leap out of the chair and bolt into the hallway. Mrs. Kelly says, "Hello and welcome," and sounds like she means it. She matter-of-factly hands me a copy of the *Harbrace Handbook* and tells me what page the class is reviewing.

* * *

It would be a vast oversimplification to say that I find—in the *Harbrace Handbook* or Mrs. Kelly's class or my new home—everything I need to leave the chaos of my former life behind. I yearn for my mother, not her presence, exactly, but the hope that she will say, "I'm sorry." I miss my sister, who is making her way in and out of places that are much less kind than the place I am living. I don't miss my mother's husband, or their house. I do miss disappearing, as strange as that may seem. I really miss cigarettes.

Even so, the reality of my life, for the first time in a long time, is this: a hot breakfast, school, afternoon snack, homework, dinner, bed. Concrete nouns, rock solid and reliable. Abstract nouns: safety, peace. Sometimes I wake up breathless from nightmares, but I am not alone. The woman who becomes the mother to my true self listens out for me at night. She walks softly, on the balls of her feet, holding her housecoat to keep it from rustling, so as not to startle me. I do not realize until months later that I never hear her leave; she hums and rubs my back where the knots have formed between my shoulder blades, until I fall asleep.

* * *

In Mrs. Kelly's class, second period, Monday through Friday, we continue our journey through the *Harbrace Handbook*. I am pretty good at grammar, as it turns out. Although my classmates seem to struggle with discerning where sentences begin and end, I easily spot independent and subordinate clauses. I make verb tenses consistent and steady them, keep them from veering between present and past. Moody, I speak to myself in the interrogative, dream of confronting my mother and her husband and all the people who looked the other way in the imperative. I devour stacks of books, struck by how the sentences arc and peak, ebb and flow, each seductive stack of words building a powerful tower of meaning. Nouns can be subject as well as object. Pronouns and antecedents agree in number and person, no clashes, no confrontations. Verbs create action in sentences, in many forms: infinitive, participle past and present, future, conditional. To live. I cried. I am learning. I will laugh. If I forget…

Another joy of Mrs. Kelly's class, I must confess, is watching the absurdly muscled members of the football squad sweat through the verbal grammar drills, the ones I navigate with ease.

"Please identify the dangling modifier, Mr. Ackerman." Mrs. Kelly points to an obvious flaw in the sentence on the board.

"Dang!" says Mr. Ackerman.

"No, sir. That's an interjection."

"Ha! The tie guy!!!" I scribble lines of exclamation points in my notebook.

I also smile to myself when Mrs. Kelly emphasizes the intimate and unalterable relationship between passing grades in English and the ability to play football for the mighty Fighting Patriots. On the outside I am still tongue-tied, the quietest member of the class who speaks only when commanded, which Mrs. Kelly does, with unnerving regularity. At the same time, I begin to like some of my other classes. I find a few other misfits to eat lunch with; I walk home in the brisk wind and feel strength returning to my arms and legs. My shoulder aches, but it is healing, and I can hug my new father. I don't remember when I realize that I am leading a regular life, looking forward to meals with my family, to the predictable routine of homework and chores. I especially anticipate Mrs. Kelly's class, where I work my way from collective nouns to transitive and intransitive verbs, to case and mood, to the vast wealth of punctuation: comma breath, semicolon pause, full stop, exclaim, query. I open the eyes of the squinting modifiers, rescue those precariously dangling, scoop up the misplaced ones, and gently—almost reverently—put them back where they belong.

In that front row, listening to the tense breathing of the defensive linemen seated behind me, I begin to learn not only the conventions of grammar but also the rules of possibility: I remember my days and sleep through most of my nights; after school, I go to my home, and no one there strikes or screams. There is a quiet consistency that, on occasion, bores me but more often leads me into dreaming about what can be.

A flock of kiting birds. A class of eager students. A team of terrified Patriots. A family of peaceable people. We soar. We learn. We quake. We live.

BETH RICHARDS's work has appeared in Fourth Genre *(Editor's Prize),* Solstice Literary Magazine, Talking Writing, *and the* Cincinnati Review *(Robert and Adele Schiff Award); in two anthologies—*Coming Out in the South *and* Into Sanity—*and in Michael Steinberg's blog (#84, "Stories and Stars"). She is a Florida native who migrated north and (much later) earned an MFA from the Solstice MFA in Creative Writing Program (Lasell University).*

Margaret Adams

Ellen answered her phone on the third ring. "Hi, how is it?" she said. She knew it was Gina without looking at the screen. Ellen would have picked up sooner, but she'd tossed her cell into her bottom desk drawer when she'd first arrived at the clinic at four in the morning, turning off the building's security alarm and letting herself in hours before the workday technically started. She'd jumped at the ringing in the still-silent office and had to fish it back out. She could never sleep when Gina was out of town.

"I'm halfway between Belfast and Blue Hill," Gina said. It was almost ten in the morning where she was. Her voice was tight. "The snow is coming down hard."

Ellen could picture the road, and from the timbre of the other woman's voice, she could picture Gina's knuckles white on the steering wheel. She had a moment of vertigo-inducing doubling: she was sitting in a desk chair in a clinic in the city, but she could also so easily picture the swirl of snow. She thought, *Get the fuck off the phone if it's so bad, then*, but she didn't say that, because she could tell Gina was already freaking and didn't need any more of that energy. Instead Ellen shut her eyes and tried to remember the exact turns in that stretch of the road, tried to will the snowflakes to be beautiful and not terrifying and to project that calm into her voice.

"How is the road itself?" Ellen asked. "Is it icy? Is the snow sticking?"

"No. The road isn't that bad, actually, I'm just going very, very slowly because it's so hard to *see*."

"Can you follow a plow or a truck?"

"There's no one else out here," Gina said. She really did sound terrible.

"Okay. Well, at least the road is okay. And you're driving towards the coast, towards towns with more money, which means the road is going to get better, better built and better maintained." Ellen was just making stuff up, but she knew that was what Gina called her for. Ellen was the kind of person who you called when you needed someone to make stuff up that would make you feel better.

"Right. Good. Okay," Gina said. Then she started to talk about everything else that was scaring her. The snow, but more than that, the entire homebirth that Sarah-Beth and Leslie had planned, the reason why she was driving to their hometown in the middle of January in the first place. The distance between their house and the closest hospital. The midwife's two-wheel-drive car. The supplies that, she had just found out, midwives weren't allowed to carry in Maine. "What kind of bullshit is that, anyway, that you aren't allowed to carry Methergine outside of the hospital?" Gina said. "Do they think we're going to start doing kitchen-counter abortions with it? What if there's a postpartum hemorrhage? And what if Sarah-Beth needs an emergency C-section but we can't get to the hospital because of the snow?"

"It'll be okay," Ellen said, though her own stomach was knotting with every sentence. "Don't panic about stuff that hasn't happened yet. These are the things you're always scared about with every birth. And most of the time everything is totally fine, would be fine even if no one was there at all. You've been the doula for plenty of home births. What's the difference this time? Just the snow. Just that one thing. Nothing else has gotten more dangerous. Plus Sarah-Beth is a midwife. Not that she'll be able to help in her own birth, but she knows what she's doing, risk-wise. She's making her own choices."

"You're right. Okay," she said. Through the phone line Ellen could hear Gina breathe in, and back out. When she spoke next her tone had shifted to one with increased clarity and a slightly lower pitch. She wasn't venting any more. She was managing. "You're doing seizure watch tonight, right? Last night was Michael?"

"Yup. We've got it."

"Okay. Thank you. I'm going to focus on driving now."

"Good," Ellen said. "I love you."

"Love you too." She hung up.

Ellen kept the phone to her ear for another moment, trying to keep manifesting her mental image of calm: snow falling but not sticking yet, the tires of the rental car catching the pavement nice and easy. She'd wanted to say, *Text me when you get there.* But Gina was going to two other women who needed her, who would be expecting her, who would know to call someone if she didn't make it in time.

Ellen tucked the phone back into her desk drawer, but then felt like it was too far away, so she shoved it into the top of her boot.

She busied herself with the stack of patient records on her desk. She'd just cleaned out the paper box a day or two ago; how was it so full again? She signed papers without reading them, forms for physical therapy, forms for approving diabetic supplies, lancets and test strips, *continue with current standing orders,* sign sign sign, fax. Then she pulled out the records she'd requested and now should really read, stacks of medical histories too thick for binder clips, held together loosely with oversized rubber bands instead. A patient who told her he had no medical problems had, per his previous doctor, had a stent placed two years earlier. What was so wrong with all of them, her, the patients, the systems, that *this* was how she found that out, by wading through paperwork after several months of being his medical provider? Did he think, after the stent was placed, *That went well, I guess it's better now, no need to tell my next provider about it?* That it was no longer a "problem"? What was wrong with how she asked patients questions, anyway, with how she did—or in this case didn't—examine them, that she hadn't figured this out before now? She went through his previous lab results with a highlighter and a pen, his previous medications, formulations tried and failed, the field notes of the ongoing experiment that was Western medicine vs. Mr. Jones.

Her coworkers started coming in and saying *good morning*, and she was startled, both because she'd been alone in the clinic for hours, and because it was *still*, after all this time, technically morning. "Hey." She swiveled her chair towards a colleague, held up the stack of papers. "Mr. Jones who swore he had no chronic medical problems had a stent and two myocardial infarctions."

The coworker laughed. "Typical," he said. "I mean, what's a *problem*, really."

"Right," Ellen said. "I should put 'Optimist' on his chronic conditions list."

Her phone buzzed and she jumped, grabbed it. It was a text from Gina's husband Josh, confirming that Ellen was coming over for seizure watch that night. Ellen read the message, replied, then shoved the phone back into her boot.

The front doors of the community health center opened and from nine until noon she saw patients every fifteen minutes. *Good morning, what can I do for you today, Good morning, what brings you in today, Hello, how have you been?* Every time, she made a point to add, early on: *I'm expecting an important phone call from a colleague, so I just want to apologize in advance if I have to step out.* Gina was kind of a colleague, she thought. It was kind of work.

Another text buzzed in. *I got here safely.* Of course Gina texted her.

*   *   *

Gina's husband Josh had seizures, but only in his sleep, his brain firing uncontrollably a few times every year as he switched between REM cycles. He couldn't be alone at night as a result, so if Gina ever left town, someone had to be around Josh at night. Often, it was Ellen, who slept on their couch with a baby monitor, ready to give him meds if he seized. The fact that this only happened to Josh in his sleep was both a blessing and a curse. It meant he could still drive, but that napping was a hazard he could not afford. He had to be especially careful not to nod off on long plane rides, pinching himself or listening to bad loud music to stay awake.

"You're like a shark," Ellen said after he let her into the apartment that evening, "who can't stop swimming, or it'll die. Or like Tony Stark in Iron Man, whose arc reactor is simultaneously keeping him alive and slowly poisoning him with palladium."

"Or just like a normal human being, whose pursuit of basic needs is a nightly act of biologic fulfillment, except on those few occasions when my own brain tries to kill me."

"That's dark."

He shrugged. He was worried about Gina and the snow, too.

They ate takeout directly out of paper cartons on the coffee table. Josh and Ellen didn't spend that much time together without Gina, but enough so that it wasn't weird when they did. They read their books and Josh put on a series of records. He drank a beer, and Ellen used their kettle to make herself tea. Ellen wanted a beer, too, but she didn't drink anymore when she was on seizure watch. She flipped through one of Gina's science magazines. *Self-destructive microbe species can commit ecological suicide,* the headline read. *Certain microbes make their environments unliveably toxic and wipe themselves out.*

Relatable, Ellen thought.

Ellen never went back to their hometown anymore, but she was glad Gina did and brought back the news, glad that she, Ellen, could be with Josh and make it easier for Gina to go anywhere at all. Ellen wanted to hear about how Sarah-Beth was doing. She missed Sarah-Beth, and was excited for her even if she shared Gina's homebirth nerves.

Sarah-Beth and her wife Leslie had always planned for Sarah-Beth to have a homebirth. The last time Ellen had seen Sarah-Beth, she'd just had her second miscarriage, and they'd been drinking the least festive margaritas Ellen had ever had, which was saying something. Sarah-Beth's voice was bitter as she'd talked. "I'm a gold-star girl. Did you know that?" she'd said suddenly. "I'm thirty years old and I've never slept with a man. I thought my body would encounter sperm for the first time and *boom*, pregnant. But no. Or it does and then I can't *stay* pregnant. I don't understand." She'd started crying.

Ellen had handed her a cocktail napkin. "Hey, hey," she'd said. "I thought you wanted your margarita unsalted."

Sarah-Beth had laughed through her tears. "I just want you to know, Ellen, that I've never thought you were an asshole. Don't listen to what anyone else says. You're just awkward as fuck."

Who says I'm an asshole? Ellen thought but did not say.

That was two years ago, before Sarah-Beth had stopped talking to her, too.

Now Ellen set her book down on the couch next to her. A margarita sounded good, even an unsalted, sad one. Or any one of the beers that she had unwillingly counted in their fridge: four, on the bottom shelf in the back. She checked the weather report for back home. Snow was still coming down.

*   *   *

The one time Josh had a seizure while Ellen was staying over, it was one-thirty in the morning. Gina was away at a bachelorette party. Ellen had been drinking, and it took her longer than it should have to respond. She'd thought it would be okay to have a few drinks with Josh that evening. It wasn't like she was *at work*. Then after he went to bed, she couldn't sleep, so she got up and had a few more.

When Josh seized, she wasn't sure if, or for how long, she'd been asleep. Didn't know, at first, what she was hearing. She was on the floor, not the couch, when she became aware that something was happening, something outside of her own head. She was supposed to set a timer when he started to seize, but she forgot, and she had no idea how long the seizure—because it *was* a seizure, she knew that now—had been going on. Had she never turned on the monitor? She stumbled into their bedroom.

Gina had warned Ellen that the hardest part of taking care of Josh during a seizure was physically wrestling him into place in order to give him ten milligrams of diazepam. Ellen was strong, she could do that, fine. What she wasn't prepared for was how violent it felt. Josh bleated and thrashed while Ellen pinned his legs down. This wasn't a hospital bed with anonymous sheets and a railing that Ellen could operate with familiar, clinical remove. It was Gina and Josh's apartment, their bed, with one of Gina's dumb tapestries from college hanging on the wall. The room revolved around her and Ellen cried with her mouth open and she didn't check the dosage until after she'd already administered it.

Josh stopped seizing as Ellen called 911. Then a minute later—that fast? she wasn't sure, she had the spins—Ellen let six paramedics into the apartment.

Josh was surprisingly cogent. Gina had warned Ellen that he would be, warned her he'd seem totally fine and not to believe him. Josh's postictal states, that period between the seizure subsiding and returning to his normal self, were famously misleading. Once he had insisted on buying a bunch of records right after a seizure and then, six hours later, had found the pile and asked what idiot had bought such bad records. The paramedics kept looking at Ellen, not Josh, and Ellen struggled to look sober while trying to explain the situation. "He has nocturnal epilepsy," she said. "He had a seizure. I already gave him diazepam."

"You're his wife?"

"No, I'm a friend who stays over in case this happens—in case he has a seizure. I'm a nurse practitioner."

"So you're his nurse?" asked the same paramedic. He was the one in charge. Or maybe he was just the tallest. She thought there had been six of them, but suddenly she only saw five, and they were all staring at her.

"I'm his wife's best friend," Ellen said. "I stay here while she's out of town in case he has a seizure. I'm also a nurse practitioner. I already gave him ten milligrams of diazepam." She thought maybe she was repeating herself.

They turned to Josh. "Can you tell us your name, sir?"

"Joshua."

"What month is it?"

"January."

"Do you know what happened?"

"It does seem likely that I had a seizure. That's usually why there are suddenly paramedics in my bedroom."

"Who is this woman over here?"

"That's Ellen."

"Who is she?"

"She's… she's just Ellen."

"Do you know why we're here?"

Josh rolled his eyes in a way that was reassuringly Josh-like and not mid-seizure-like. "I supposed you've all come over to have a jam session. Let's get out the amps," he said.

The paramedics all looked at Ellen. "He's very sarcastic," she said. "That's normal."

"Josh-o, Joshy, Josh-y-oh, my man," said one of the paramedics, and both Josh and Ellen winced. "Who's the president?"

"Barack Obama."

They were all quiet.

"Right?" Josh said.

"Josh," Ellen said from the corner. "Prime numbers."

"2, 3, 5, 7, 11, 13, 17."

"Who's the president?"

"Barack Obama."

The paramedics shuffled. One of them turned to Ellen. "Ma'am, do you feel comfortable if we don't transport him to the hospital and leave him here with you? You think he's okay?"

"Yeah, that's fine," Ellen said. "I think he's okay." They picked up their gear and filed out of the apartment.

Ellen sat cross-legged at the bottom of the bed, a discrete distance away from where Josh leaned against the headboard. She wondered if it was an intrusion for her to be sitting on the bed at all. Maybe it was good that she was drunk.

"I didn't bite my tongue that badly," he said, moving his mouth experimentally. Then his face reassembled stubbornness. "Who's the president?" he asked.

Ellen just looked at him.

"Look, I can tell I keep whiffing that question. Who is it?"

"I don't think I'm supposed to tell you, I think I'm supposed to wait until it comes back to you to make sure your brain is doing everything right."

"Come on. Just tell me."

Outside, the streetlights shone against the blinds. "It's Trump," she said.

He looked at her, then flopped back against the pillows. "Fuck. Right. Well. That's sobering."

This was the thing that they laughed about, eventually, later. It was nowhere near morning yet. He'd never had a seizure this early in the night before, and Ellen wasn't supposed to let him go back to sleep, but it was barely 2am, and she was so tired. Ellen kept him awake for an hour by asking him to explain how synthesizers worked. Then she let him go back to sleep.

He seized again within forty-five minutes. He bit his tongue badly that time, and blood poured over his face. Ellen gave him the only dose of diazepam that was left—was he even allowed to have two doses in one night? Had she done that math right?—and she called 911 again. This time Ellen told the paramedics that something was really wrong, that he never had two seizures in a single night, though of course, he'd never been allowed to go back to sleep after a seizure, either, though she didn't say that part. She swept Josh and Gina's entire medicine cabinet into her backpack, not trusting herself to read the labels, and followed them into the ambulance.

At the hospital, the nurses asked Josh again who the president was and checked his blood sugar for the fifth time. "Barack Obama," Josh said. He looked sad. He could tell he was getting it wrong.

Ellen nodded off in the visitor's chair next to Josh's hospital bed while they monitored him. As she slowly sobered up, she got more horrified. Suddenly, she wasn't sure: had he had two seizures, or three? She remembered how slow she'd been to rouse. How she hadn't even been sure how many paramedics were in the room. She vomited in the medical waste bin in the corner of the hospital bay and the nurses had all glared at her and checked Josh's blood alcohol level (normal) again.

Ellen couldn't stop remembering the horrible sounds Josh had made while he was seizing, how it had felt, in the moment, like she was hurting him.

After Josh had been discharged from the hospital and Gina had come home, Ellen didn't talk to them for three weeks, because she was pretty sure she had nearly killed Josh.

*   *   *

Now Ellen made it through the night with her herbal tea, but she barely slept. In the morning she moved around Gina and Josh's apartment shakily. It was getting harder and harder to sleep on their couch, and she'd been up half of the night. She made coffee for her and Josh and pretended to be okay. She checked the weather again to see how the snowstorm back home was developing.

Two hours into her workday, between her 10:45 and 11am patients, Ellen got a text from Gina. *Looks like I'm delivering a baby*, she said. *We're snowed in, the midwife is snowed in, Sarah is 7 cm dilated and her water just broke.* Ellen called her immediately, but Gina didn't pick up and didn't send any more texts.

Then Ellen had an idea that she immediately regretted, not because it was a bad idea, but because she didn't want to do it, and having thought it, she really should do it. She picked up her phone and typed a name into the contacts with her thumb. Horribly, she had not deleted his number.

He picked up on the fourth ring. "Hello?"

"Hey, Matt," she said. "It's Ellen!"

There was a long pause.

"How's it going?" Ellen said.

More silence. Then he said, "Are you in a program? On step nine? Are you step-nining me?"

She laughed. He didn't. "No," she said. "Um. Do you still live in Sedgewick? And do you still have a plow?"

There was silence on the other end of the line.

"I'm asking because Sarah-Beth is about to have a home birth in Blue Hill, not that far from you? And they're snowed in? And so is their midwife? And maybe, you could plow them all out."

Ellen's medical assistant came around the corner and handed her a filled-out intake form. She mouthed *room four* at Ellen with large accompanying hand signals including four fingers and some okay signs before disappearing back into the main area of the clinic. When Matt spoke next his voice was flat. "You're calling me because you want me to go out in a blizzard and plow people out as a favor."

"Yep. That's the long and short of it." She laughed again but she was not really trying this time and it sounded awful.

"Text me the address," he said. "But I'm not doing it for you. And you know, I felt better about this when I thought you were step-nining me." He hung up.

Ellen took what she mentally thought of as *three deep yoga breaths*, which would be more helpful if she actually did yoga, then jumped up and down a few times like a human Etch A Sketch. She looked at the intake form her assistant had just handed her. Under "chief concern today" her next patient had written "anxiety." Ellen texted Sarah-Beth's address to Matt, then texted Gina to say he would be over to plow them out shortly. Then she went in to see her patient.

Ellen was just finishing her afternoon patients when her phone buzzed. It was Gina. *The plow guy came and things have slowed down and the midwife says she's coming.*

Ellen wanted to ask her if the plow guy had gotten fat or if he mentioned whether or not he had a girlfriend, but she knew, she *knew*, this was not the time.

A few hours later Ellen texted, *is there a baby yet?*
No, no baby yet. In transition.

*   *   *

Ellen started going to meetings after the night Josh seized, but the meetings were for adult children of alcoholics. She didn't talk about why she was really there. In the absence of actual stories about actual alcoholic parents, Ellen told stories that could have come from a patient report. Every time she showed up, strangers—a possible thing in this big city—introduced themselves, shook her hand, welcomed her, told her to keep coming back. "You're lucky you started coming so young," the older ones said, though already in her thirties, Ellen didn't feel young.

"It's just something I've been thinking about," she'd say back. "You know, the patterns you get from your families of origin. I'm a healthcare worker. I'm here more as a preventive maintenance thing. I'm lucky that I've never had a problem myself, but I want to make sure I understand the role alcohol has played in my family and in my life."

She didn't tell them why she'd left home in the first place. She didn't tell them that she sometimes had three, four, five drinks alone at night.

She didn't tell them that she wasn't even sure how many drinks she'd had the night she might not have heard her best friend's husband have a seizure. She didn't tell them that she'd been close to blacking out the time she injected him with benzodiazepines before even checking the dose.

*   *   *

Ellen stayed three hours late at work finishing her notes and when she finally walked outside it was dark already. She walked by a dive bar that she and Gina used to frequent, back when they first moved to this city, before Gina and Josh got married, before Ellen had passed her boards. Ellen had been burning her bridges slower then. She hadn't yet gotten to what Sarah-Beth, when they were still talking, referred to as her *ramming speed*. She hadn't wrecked her mother's car yet. Hadn't hooked up with Matt's brother over that same bad New Year's back home. *Everyone makes mistakes*, Gina said. *Besides, you've never hurt me, and I judge people by how they are with me, not by what other people say about them.* Gina trusted her. Ellen looked through the bar window and chewed her right pinky nail hard enough that she could taste blood from the cuticle. Ellen had been telling herself for a while, now, that she could stop drinking without anyone knowing. She was a grown woman. A healthcare professional. Just today, she'd had three office visits with patients she'd counseled on their substance use. Motivational interviewing.

Stages of change. She was willing to do the work as long as no one had to know. She turned away from the window and kept walking, quickly, to Gina and Josh's apartment.

At three in the morning that night, having finally dozed off with the help of melatonin gummies and still more herbal tea, Ellen jerked awake. She was on her feet, every startle response engaged, her heart pounding. But no, it wasn't Josh, it wasn't a seizure, it was only her phone that had made a sound. She'd gotten a text from Gina: a picture of Sarah-Beth, Leslie, and a new baby. Everyone looked whole and tiredly happy. Slowly, Ellen sank back down onto the couch. *HURRAY,* she texted back. The thing was done and everyone looked okay.

But it hadn't been okay. Gina would tell her, later, how it went. She would tell her that the midwife arrived late, just twenty minutes before Sarah-Beth delivered, and that the midwife's assistant never made it at all. That Sarah-Beth had a separation of the placenta and lost a liter of blood while the midwife pounded her abdomen with her fist, trying to get her uterus to contract without Methergine. That Gina had to resuscitate the baby.

Gina would tell Ellen all this later while they stared at each other from opposite ends of her kitchen table. Ellen would tell Gina that she had done everything right.

"Be careful," Gina would say, taking even but shallow breaths as she laid out the story, methodically and removed, like someone marking out lengths of rope. "I will cry if you are too nice to me right now."

After, when the baby was breathing and Sarah-Beth was no longer bleeding out and it had been determined that everyone was going to survive, Gina had fished the clots out of the tub and carried twenty gallons of bloody water into the woods. Then she had done three loads of laundry.

"There was a moment," Gina would tell Ellen several days from now. "When I was bagging the baby, trying to give her enough air but trying also not to overinflate her lungs. I was so tired, and I just thought, *I would rather be anywhere but here.* I wasn't scared any more. I was done, and I was gone. And I didn't stop bagging the baby, but you could tell. And when I looked up, Sarah-Beth was looking right at me, and I knew she'd seen, that at the worst moment, I had left them."

And when Gina tells Ellen this, two days from now, Ellen will start to say, *That's crazy.* Ellen will start to say, *She was bleeding out after twelve hours of labor in a blizzard and you had a neonatal resuscitation mask on her newborn; I'm absolutely sure she didn't see into your quote-unquote seditious soul and judge you for it.* Ellen will start to say, *Sure, but you were still doing all of the things. You did everything right. Hell, they let you give the baby her middle name!* But she wouldn't say this, because it wouldn't really matter. It wouldn't really matter, and they both would know it. What would matter was Gina's story, her shaken belief in herself, and the way in which that doubt had already calcified in her brain.

But that night, knowing only that the baby had been born, holding her phone in her hand with the photo still open, Ellen didn't know any of this yet. She looked at the picture of the two exhausted mothers and the new baby, waiting for her heart rate to slow back down again. She thought about Matt, disappointed that she was not calling to make amends. About Josh, on the other side of the wall from her, courting death in his respite from the conscious mind. About Sarah-Beth, a midwife, who knew full well what birth entailed, struggling so hard to get pregnant anyway, like an engineer stepping in front of her own train. And she thought about what she, Ellen, would do next. That maybe this time she would finally tell Gina the truth when she got home, the truth about the problem Ellen was starting to understand that she had, even if that meant Gina would stop trusting her.

MARGARET ADAMS's *writing has appeared in over two dozen publications, including* The Best Small Fictions 2019, Threepenny Review, Joyland Magazine, *and* The Pinch Journal. *She lives in Vermont.*

Driftwood

Elizabeth Kleinfeld

The possibility of having hot sex was half the reason for our stay at the Art Hotel. With Denver on COVID lockdown, except for hospital stays and doctor's appointments, we hadn't left our house in months. In the kind of impulsive decision-making typical of stroke survivors, my husband Tom decided we needed to paint the entire first floor of our house, and one caregiving lesson I had learned was to choose my battles carefully.

The stroke left Tom paralyzed on his left. In our dozen years together, I had always taken care of him in some ways—cooked for him, cleaned up after him, organized our social life. But after the stroke, I trimmed his nails, including his gnarled toenails. I rubbed his feet with lotion. I helped him from his wheelchair to the toilet, and then I sat on the edge of the tub and talked to him to keep him from falling asleep or to remind him where he was and what he was doing. I bathed him and checked his delicate skin for red spots, the telltale sign of pressure sores. He was only sixty, but the stroke has rendered him fragile as a newborn.

In the days leading up to our hotel stay, I moved all the appliances off the kitchen counters, took artwork and shelves off the walls, pushed the furniture into the middle of each room, checked in with the painters to confirm they would do the ceilings. Periodically, as I buzzed around, Tom said, "Remind me again why you're doing all this?"

"We're having the house painted," I would say, sometimes reminding him: "You picked white with dark blue trim." With my low vision, I can't be trusted to pick colors.

"Oh, right," he would respond. "That's going to look great."

Sometimes he asked if it was Black Friday yet. "No," I told him, "That's the day after Thanksgiving." He was excited to do online shopping for his son and my daughter. The stroke wiped out the little bit of financial restraint he had and I froze his credit card.

"Is today Thanksgiving?" he asked.

*　*　*

Sex was always a cornerstone of our relationship. And by sex, I mean fucking. We never made love. No, we fucked, hard and fierce, each of us driven to possess and be possessed, devour and be devoured, taste and be tasted. When we fucked, we held nothing back, giving and taking with abandon in a way we never could through conversation. Our fucking was fueled by a deep hunger for connection that neither of us could express any other way. Our sex left us both sore, exhausted, and hungry for more. Neither of us ever denied the other, no matter what was going on in other parts of our marriage.

After his stroke, the desire was still there but buried beneath so many challenges we needed an excavator to find it: his limited attention span, the physical logistics of his paralyzed body, his unpredictable response to the little blue pills his doctor prescribed, and my exhaustion. We were hoping the days in the hotel would allow time and space for the excavation.

As a result of the stroke, Tom had a mysterious condition called left neglect, which made him unaware of anything happening on his left side. He read book pages starting in the middle of a line and reading to the right margin, never realizing he had missed the first half of that line. If I whispered sweet nothings into his left ear, his brain didn't process the sound. Those same sweet nothings whispered into his right ear could elicit an *oh, baby...*

The most difficult challenges had to do with his penis, which I had referred to as his cock before the stroke. During his six weeks in the hospital, it became commonplace to talk with the nursing staff about his penis as they showed me how to use the condom catheters, a catheter that fit over his penis like a condom and connected to a tube leading to a drainage bag for urine. It felt oddly clinical to discuss that most intimate of body parts as a penis. How many steamy things had I texted and said about that body part over the years without ever using the word penis? How different and starkly comical those same texts and sentiments would have been had I used the word penis.

Sometimes we laughed about this. I would say, "Oh, baby, I want your big fat..." I paused for dramatic effect. "Penis inside me."

"That's hot," Tom would say, sometimes winking at me with his right eye. Unless I had spoken into his left ear, and then he would not respond, prompting me to scurry over to his right to repeat the absurdity.

And then there was the issue of his being oddly disconnected from his body, his penis being no exception. He typically had no idea whether the arousal in his brain was exhibited in his penis—and sometimes an erection seemed to have no connection to anything in his brain. Sometimes, seeing an erection, I asked, "Are you trying to tell me something?" with a flirtatious smile. He responded with confusion as often as he did a salacious leer.

I relished every opportunity for skin-to-skin contact. For the nearly two weeks he was unable to speak because of the ventilator, I spent most of the twelve-hour visiting period each day simply holding his right hand, sometimes interweaving my fingers between his, other times holding his hand in my two, running my fingers over the knuckles and in the valleys between each finger. Over and over, I kissed his palm, his wrist, I breathed in deeply the smell of the skin between his thumb and index finger. I rubbed his feet each night with a eucalyptus lotion he loved, stroking the soles slowly and deliberately, my entire body engaged. When he came home, I continued rubbing his feet at night. After bathing him, I rubbed a different lotion on his limbs and torso, stopping to kiss the small of his back, the crook of each elbow, the base of his cock.

*   *   *

Our first full day at the hotel begins like many at home. Just after 5am, I wake to hear Tom saying urgently, "Babe, hey, Babe. I've got a leak." The condom catheters are maddeningly imperfect. The adhesive that makes the condom stick to his penis could fail, the condom could break, the joint between the condom and the line to the bag could give out, the line could get kinked, leading to a backup that would rupture the condom, the bag itself could leak. We have experienced all of this.

Still groggy and disoriented, I get out of bed and pull over his wheelchair.

"Let's get you into the chair so I can change the sheets."

In my hurry to get him out of the wet bedding, I start pulling him into a sitting position in the bed by his shoulders without first announcing I would do so, which confuses him.

The dogs are alert now, moving around the room with their tails wagging, lingering by the closet where they know their breakfast and leashes are.

"I don't think my leg is going to hold up," he says. His left leg is weaker than the right and it is unclear why. Is it because he uses it less since his brain doesn't register it? Or is it just as strong as the right but he doesn't trust it because he can't communicate with it? Or perhaps he has actually injured his leg? Injuries that reveal themselves through bruises and blood are easy to verify; others, not so much.

"Let's see if you can do the transfer without the brace," I say, not wanting to take the time to put the brace that supports his ankle on. I hate the thought of him lying in wet bedding for a moment longer than necessary.

I wrap the broad gait belt, designed specifically for assisting someone with walking, around him. "Ready to stand?"

"No, my leg…" he says, but I am already pulling him up. "My ankle, my ankle," he protests. I swing him around into the wheelchair, where he plops down awkwardly. The dogs look at me with accusation in their eyes. I have done it all wrong—I haven't worked with him as a partner. I have invalidated what he told me about his leg. I dismiss the recriminations in my head; yes, I did it all wrong, but I had reasons.

"I'm sorry," I say, wiping his legs and crotch down with a washcloth. "I just want to get you out of the wet bedding." My mind frantically calculates all that has to be done—get him into his chair, get his wet pajama pants off him, change his Depends, wipe him down, get clean pants on him—that will involve two stands—get clean bedding, make the bed, move him back into bed. The dogs need to be walked and fed, no, fed then walked. Tom needs his drugs. I need to wash my face and pull my hair back before I can think straight.

I call the front desk to ask for a new set of sheets. I realize I'd been on his left and he hasn't processed that I've made the call when I step back into his field of vision and he says, "I don't know where you've been, but I have a situation." He holds out his phone.

"See what's on there. I've been getting texts all night. This guy Carlos from the mansion needs money." The mansion was the historic home remodel he worked on as a foreman before the stroke. Carlos was an electrician.

"What do you mean he needs money?" I ask, glad I froze his credit cards.

"I think he's running for president… in Venezuela maybe? He needs money." I look at his phone. There are no new texts, nothing from anyone named Carlos. I search to see which apps he's used recently. *Instagram.* I open it—there's a video posted by someone named Carlos at a street protest. I don't think it's the Carlos Tom knows. I try to explain to him that the video isn't of his friend.

His right brow furrows. "Please, Babe, I need you to trust me on this. Carlos needs money; he's in trouble in Venezuela. And I'm worried about my leg. There's nothing left in it and it's still early." His agitation escalates suddenly. "Call the front desk about the bedding."

"I did," I snap. "I was on your left. You didn't see me."

He doesn't acknowledge that I've said anything.

"Well then where's the goddamn bedding?" he finally says.

Before I can answer, he says, "Call the front desk again. They forgot about us." The dogs pace and eye me warily.

"It's only been like five minutes," I say, but he cuts me off.

"They fucking forgot about us. Call them, tell them to hurry."

I don't respond. I feed the dogs and go to the bathroom. I look at my face in the mirror—frizzy hair, splotchy skin. I haven't had a haircut since the pandemic began and am six months overdue. I shake my head and sigh, pulling my awful hair back into a ponytail and splashing cold water on my face. I can't change my appearance. Like many things in my life right now, it is what it is.

The sheets finally arrive and I change the bedding. "Do you want to get back into bed?"

"Yes," he says, his voice flat with exhaustion.

*   *   *

I get the dogs leashed up and out—130 pounds between them of antsy, pent-up energy. With the pandemic, the streets are eerily empty. The sidewalk is uneven, with things my low vision doesn't pick up randomly scattered. I struggle with differentiating items of similar colors—a black metal fence in front of a black building is invisible to me. I find myself kicking paper cups and discarded masks. Excited by the smells, the dogs pull at their leashes, barking and lunging at the occasional chunk of food on the sidewalk. My mind is blurred in panic. Is Tom's confusion and anxiety what the future holds? What if he can never again get out of bed or put on his shirt without my help? What if it's all on me for the rest of our lives? How can I possibly take care of Tom, the dogs, myself?

Something tangles around my foot, and I lurch awkwardly into the grass. The dogs bound over to me. "We're not fucking playing!" I bark at them. My heart thumps in my chest—what if I had actually been injured?

I haven't even had any coffee yet.

I need to talk to someone who can pull me back from this ledge I feel like I'm on. My mind cycles through who I can call. With the pandemic, it seems everyone's life is in chaos and I don't want to add to it. My sister has enough on her plate, suddenly homeschooling her son. I call my friend Lunden; she answers immediately. I'm crying as I tell her I don't know how to take care of Tom or myself.

"Of course you don't, honey. You've never had to do this before. You were thrown into this. But you're resourceful and smart. You'll be okay. Take a deep breath and tell me what happened."

She reminds me to breathe, to take things one at a time. I tell her the Venezuela thing is Tom's reality and she says, "Okay, so humor him. Tell him you've emailed the guy with support." She makes it sound so simple.

The deep breaths help. It will be okay.

I take another deep breath. I chant *nam myoho renge kyo*, the Buddhist expression of the mystic law: suffering can be overcome through faith in karma. I chant for love and strength for Tom and myself. I close my eyes and say out loud, "I trust the universe."

By the time I get back to the hotel room with the dogs, I feel calm. Tom is drowsing in bed, but when he hears us come in, he calls out, "Hey, Babe, can I get some coffee?" I don't know if he remembers the chaos of earlier. I make us coffee and help him sit up and swing his legs around so he's perched on the edge of the bed. He spent weeks in PT strengthening his core muscles so he could hold himself upright in this position.

"What's on my dance card today?" he asks. His physical therapist is coming to the hotel for a session with him. I participate in all of his PT sessions so I can learn how to help him walk, sit, stand, and balance between sessions. After PT, Tom is wiped out and sleeps for hours. I manage to rouse him for dinner, which he nibbles on before falling asleep again.

Despite my trusting the universe, there will be no hot sex today.

* * *

"I can't find my goddamn wallet." Tom is talking in his sleep. I ask him what he's talking about, but I'm lying to his left and he's sound asleep anyway.

In the morning he tells me, "I had a dream about going to one of the diners around here for a burrito, but now I remember that I can't do that." He's been dreaming of walking.

Hot sex will have to wait: Today we have timed-entry tickets into the art museum a block away. Because of the isolation of COVID and my thinking that getting out and doing things will help us acclimate to Tom's physical limitations, I got the tickets to force us out.

I notice there's hardly any liquid in his pee bag. He's dehydrated. When he was in the rehab unit, the staff explained to me that the battery of a person who's had a stroke runs down quickly and every little thing that goes wrong—disrupted sleep, dehydration—plus expended effort and cognitive load run it down faster. I try to remember if he drank his usual amount of fluids yesterday. I wonder if he held back because of the catheter blow out. I'll push fluid today.

I am intimately aware of his body's every nuance. His urine output, his bowel movements, his talking in his sleep, where the sweat collects on his body, the spot on the bottom of his left foot that is susceptible to the pressure of his shoes and turns red by the end of every day.

Tom grumbles when I tell him it's time to start getting ready to head to the museum. Since the stroke, he is perpetually cold and getting him to go outside always involves me promising and reaffirming multiple times that I will bundle him up. It is fifty-five degrees and sunny, but he insists on long underwear, adding ten minutes onto our routine. I get him into his wheelchair.

"Where's my super sweet skull cap?" he asks. He wants the warmth but also to hide the jagged scar that marks the wedge of skull that was removed to give his brain room to swell after the stroke.

Because of COVID, the museum is strictly limiting entry. They check our tickets before waving us into the lobby. This is the first time we've been somewhere with Tom using the wheelchair beyond a doctor's office or hospital. It's uncharted territory. First the hotel, now a museum! Nothing can stop us now!

Except that when we get to the portrait exhibit, the doors into the gallery are not equipped with an automatic opener, so I have to hold the door open with my butt, turn around to face Tom in his wheelchair, and pull his chair forward.

The gallery is dark—the walls navy and the lights low with each portrait illuminated by its own light. Because of the carefully modulated entry into the museum, there are very few people in the gallery. I can push Tom's wheelchair slowly, with the portraits to his right, and he tells me when he wants to linger over a piece. I am grateful for our slow pace because it is so hard for me to see in the gallery. I have to walk right up to the placards on the walls to read them, my nose just a few inches away, sometimes using my cell phone's flashlight for extra illumination.

We have camped and rafted together a hundred times but looking at artwork together is new. The same pieces get our attention. The first piece we gravitate to is Andrea Soldi's portrait of the gentleman Thomas Sheppard. It's a large oil painting from 1733, nearly five feet tall, in an ornately carved gold frame. Sheppard sports an extravagantly embroidered velvet topcoat over a gold silk waistcoat, his powdered wig extending beyond his shoulders.

"A man could really strut his stuff back then," Tom observes.

"It reminds me of your Willy Wonka Halloween costume," I say, remembering his purple finery, and he nods..

An even larger oil painting, a family portrait by Thomas Hudson from 1742, transfixes us next. A massive eight feet tall and thirteen feet wide, it shows the Radcliffes and their children, decked out in decadent eighteenth-century aristocratic fashions. Despite their restrictive clothes, the children are shown playing with toys and each other. The best part, way over on the left, is a brown and white spaniel with his paws on the lap of a little girl in a splendid dress.

"Oh, look at the dog!" I say.

"What dog?" Tom asks, and I realize it's too far on his left for him to process. I reposition his wheelchair so the dog is directly in front of him.

"Oh, look at the little guy! He's a member of the family," Tom says with glee.

But it's a tiny piece that really gets our attention: a small oval not even a foot tall. In the middle of a ring of stained glass with fleurs-de-lis and geometric designs is a bearded man's face, with downcast eyes that remind me of Tom's left eye. The note hanging on the wall next to it says it is from fifteenth-century England.

"It looks like you!" I say and turn his wheelchair so he's facing the piece head on.

"Look at that!" Tom says.

I put my face up to the placard to read it. "It's called *Head of a Bearded Man,* possibly *Jesus.*" I emphasize the *possibly* dramatically. "It's possibly Jesus. It could be anyone, but they put that possibly in front of Jesus and now you can't argue with it."

I read him the placard description: "'This piece of stained glass is composed of a head *thought to represent Jesus.*'" I emphasize the speculative part of the description. "I'm going to take a picture of you and call it *Picture of a Bearded Man, possibly Jesus.*" I hold up my phone and Tom poses, doing his best to look regal. "There, you're possibly Jesus in a mask."

"And you're possibly Mary Magdalene," he replies, his low gravelly voice slower since the stroke but still able to stir something deep inside me. We went as Jesus and Mary Magdalene to a Halloween party a few years ago. Waking up the next morning and observing our torn costumes strewn about, Tom said, "If there was a god, we'd have been smote last night."

I look at Tom's masked face in the low light, the smile crinkles showing only around his right eye and the left eye fixed in a neutral gaze. I put my hand on his right shoulder, feeling the heat of his body even through all the layers of fabric. He places his right hand on top of mine and looks at me, then puts his right hand out in front of him. I place both my hands in his, his one hand large enough to envelop both of mine. This has always been a gesture of love for us. My two hands protected within his. My breathing shifts and I feel my face flush.

*   *   *

Outside the portrait exhibit is a mezzanine, the walls covered with Shantell Martin's exuberant line drawings. The swooping, energetic doodles, full of loops and undulating lines, mesmerize us. One wall has *FIND WHAT MAKES YOU YOU INSIDE* in giant, capital letters. Tom points to it and asks what it says. I read the words aloud and he says, "Take my picture in front of that." He poses, giving a thumbs up with his right hand.

The floor on the mezzanine is smooth poured concrete and pushing his wheelchair is easy. As we glide toward the elevator, I do some loops and squiggles, mimicking the lines of Martin's work.

I push the down button and we wait in front of the two elevators. When one opens up, a small group hustles into it quickly. I am shocked. We were there first! They just took an elevator from a guy in a wheelchair!

"Those fuckers took the elevator possibly meant for Jesus!" Tom exclaims. But moments later, the other elevator opens and we realize we've scored. Unlike the first one, which was just a plain old elevator inside, this one has Shantell Martin's drawings covering the walls and ceiling. As I roll Tom in, he says, "Oh, yeah. Those fuckers missed out." I take a picture of him looking smug with the energetic squiggles behind him.

"I call this one *Man in the Elevator Possibly Meant for Jesus.*"

When the elevator delivers us to the ground floor, Tom says, "Let's check out the gift shop." As I wheel Tom around, he grabs things from shelves and displays, piling them on his lap: bookends, an origami kit, coasters.

We leave the museum shop with all of Tom's booty and head back to the room. The afternoon is already spoken for. Tom has OT and speech therapy. The afternoon and evening pass in a happy, relaxed glow.

After I get him into bed, I curl up against him. I'm on his left, but my arm drapes across his body and I nestle my hand into the warm soft space between his neck and shoulder. "Can you feel that?" I ask.

"I feel your hand, Baby," he says. "Today was a good day."

We are possibly the happiest people in the world.

*   *   *

Tom wakes up the next morning still glowing. After he drinks his coffee, he announces, "Give me a couple of those little blue pills."

I give him the pills. An hour later, I'm working at my computer and hear a clatter. I turn to see he's dropped his phone.

"Leave it," he says. "Come here."

I walk over and his big hand catches my wrist. Before his stroke, he could hold both my wrists with just one hand and use the other to pinch my nipples or finger me. Now he has to choose.

He holds my hand to his face and takes one of my fingers into his mouth. He slowly draws it out and does the same with another. I feel myself getting squirmy. He has always been irresistibly magnetic to me. I know that after his stroke, most of the world sees him as *someone in a wheelchair*, a phrase I hate for how it renders him a load to be pushed around. The wheelchair is a tool—he *uses* a wheelchair.

As he moves my fingers in and out of his mouth, he makes steady eye contact with his right eye. I feel myself melting.

"Let's go to bed," he says. I wheel him over to the bed and he says, "Take my clothes off." I do and get him into the bed, doing my best to get him close to the middle, which involves scooting his shoulders over, then his hips, and repeating that process until he's moved over a bit. He's not really in the middle, but I'm wary of exhausting us both before we get to the fun part. He tells me to take off my own clothes.

The dogs make themselves scarce. They remember how this goes from before the stroke.

I climb on top of him, my hips over his. I bend down and say softly in his right ear, "Tell me what you want." I smell the musk of his neck, his old smell of sawdust and motorcycle exhaust replaced by soap and lotion. I feel the heat radiating off his body and I begin rocking my hips against his.

"I want your nipples in my mouth," he says slowly. I sit up and arch forward. He sucks my left nipple, flicking it with his tongue, before I shift the other breast toward his mouth.

"I don't know exactly how this is going to work," I confess. He says, "Neither do I, Babe. We'll figure it out." Sex has always been the one part of our relationship we don't have to work at, but now even this is work.

I straighten up and begin grinding against him. He plants his right foot on the bed, doing his best to grind against me. "That feels good," he says and I feel his cock respond. Like the rest of him, it is muted, but there is something.

"Am I inside you?" he asks. I don't want to risk making him feel like anything less than the sexy beast I love.

"You feel so good against me." I am breathing hard, moaning. My answer seems to satisfy him.

"I want to taste you," he says, his voice thick and low.

I move forward on my knees until I am kneeling over his face. I hold onto the headboard to steady myself. His tongue probes my folds and then his fingers are inside me. I spread my legs farther, my left knee perilously close to the edge of the bed and my other one by his left arm, which lies still and I carefully avoid. I am panting.

I feel clumsy and unsure of what to do until Tom says, "Turn around." I know what he wants. I want it, too. I take his fingers into my mouth, tasting myself on him, and calculating how to turn around without hurting him. My arms and legs shake with the effort as I carefully swivel so I am facing the end of the bed, my hips hovering above his face again. I bring my face down to his crotch, breathing in his musky smell, rubbing my face into it. He moans softly and I bring him into my mouth.

His lips are gently grazing my inner thighs and then the flat of his hand is between my legs. I sit back a bit, shifting my weight into his hand, letting him feel my wetness.

I shudder involuntarily, moaning from somewhere deep inside me, and Tom says, "That's right, Baby."

After a deep breath, I return to sucking him. I want him to feel like the sexiest, most delicious man in the universe, my man, my strong brave man. There is nowhere I'd rather be than on top of him, running my tongue along his length, coaxing him to let go completely, to allow himself to be so close to me we are one. We have never been so tender with each other.

He moans softly, almost whimpering. The brief tightening and release I am used to doesn't happen, but my mouth fills with his warm, salty stickiness and I swallow it. The pungent smell of sex permeates the room and I gingerly extricate myself from him so we can nap.

He loves to feel the sun on his skin, but his eyes are sensitive to light now, so I arrange a washcloth over his eyes. We fall asleep, me on his right so he knows I'm there. I hook my top leg around his legs to keep from falling off the bed. My head rests where his chest meets his shoulder. I want to whisper to him how much I love him, but we are both exhausted from the effort and drift off into sleep, the sunshine pouring in the window, illuminating our tangled legs. The insides of my thighs are still sticky.

Something shifts in the way we touch each other after this. We are not touching to possess or capture but to invite, to explore. To share.

*   *   *

That night, Tom's leg spasms are epic. He is often woken up by intense muscle contractions. If I sleep with my head down by his feet and my arms wrapped around his calves, I can soothe the spasms a bit. Once one starts, I grab his foot with both hands, pressing on the top and bottom at the same time. The spasms stop almost immediately for a few minutes, but they don't stop coming, so we end up just waiting for the next one to hit.

Despite the tough night, Tom is in fine form for OT and PT that day.

As the session nears its end, the PT makes an offhand comment: "You'll never use the left hand the way you used to, but you might be able to gesture." Tom doesn't react and I wonder if he heard her. No one has said this to us before, and although it seems obvious that his hand will never be what it was before, I had been telling myself that with hard work, anything is possible.

After the PT leaves, I ask if he caught what she said about his hand. He says it was news to him and his tone is flat and the expression on his face inscrutable.

After a light dinner, Tom goes to bed with the dogs. I slip out of the room and go to the lobby where there is a sculpture of a horse by Deborah Butterfield, made completely of driftwood. The horse is maybe eight feet tall and appears to have a fish in its belly. The smooth, almost shiny pieces of driftwood tantalize me. I want to reach out and touch them, run my hand down the curves of the pieces that make up the horse's neck. The horse looks rugged and graceful, despite being made of wood that has been tumbled and stripped of its texture and grain. The horse presents in its sparest form, just bone, no flesh or muscle to protect it.

We are driftwood, I think, being tossed about by tumultuous waters, not knowing what shore we may wash up on. Our sharp edges are being softened, rounded. Possibly our scattered pieces will be reassembled into something new and beautiful if we trust the universe enough. I think about Tom's big, rugged, beautiful left hand, now swollen with edema. I had thought we were working hard to regain its function, but now I see that we are just treading water, working this hard to stay in place, to not lose more ground.

I look again at the beautiful driftwood horse, its neck arching gracefully, the fluidity of the legs.

I feel a gentle relief at the realization that drifting takes less effort than treading water. Nothing will ever be the way it was before. It may be better, it may be worse; all we know for sure is that it will change.

*   *   *

Our final days at the hotel are filled with PT and orthotist visits. On our last full day, Tom takes a sound afternoon nap while I grade student work. After a few hours I wake him up and make a charcuterie platter. I prop him up in bed and sit in the chair to his right, with the platter on the bed between us. I tune into a livestream concert a musician friend of mine is doing. She sings jazz tunes with piano accompaniment. Tom is radiant and upbeat.

"Delicious dinner, Babe," he says, popping a cube of cheese into his mouth. Although he's usually too tired to do anything after dinner, I decide to push my luck tonight.

"Do you want to take one more spin around the neighborhood? I'll bundle you up."

I get him dressed and into his wheelchair. From the hotel, I push him a block or two west. It's dark out now and with my vision impairment, I wonder whether this was a bad idea..

"What's that?" Tom asks, pointing to a building off to our right. There's an alcove behind it with low lighting.

As we get closer, we see stone benches and planters with late fall grasses and a stone sign indicating this is a peace garden. "It does feel peaceful," Tom says and reaches his hand out for mine. I kneel and put my head in his lap. He pets my hair. His hand feels impossibly gentle. This tender side of Tom is unfamiliar and disorienting to me, but I feel safe with my head in his lap.

Tomorrow I will shower Tom and we will go home to fresh white walls.

ELIZABETH KLEINFELD *is a writer, professor, Buddhist, and optimist living in Denver, Colorado. She is writing a memoir about being her husband's caregiver for the year before he died. Her essays about grief have been published in* The Boston Globe, Herstry, Bright Flash Literary Review, *and in an anthology about the 2020 pandemic. Her work has been nominated for the Pushcart Prize. Drawing from her experiences as both a caregiver and widow, she offers support to terminally ill patients and their families as a certified end-of-life doula. She directs the Writing Center at Metropolitan State University of Denver. Her academic work focuses on disability justice, rhetorics of oppression, and writing center pedagogy. She is currently completing certification in therapeutic journaling to help others process grief and trauma through writing. When not writing or teaching, she can be found dancing rumba, traveling,* *or experimenting with new recipes in her kitchen. Through her blog at elizabethkleinfeld.com, she explores the intersections of grief, disability, and finding joy after loss.*

SeaWorld

Aurora Huiza

Michael and I lived in the apartment our dad left us, three bedrooms in South Slope. I worked in a restaurant and won this fellowship to sculpt, an endowment from some millionaire's wife, a Russian woman named Kitty Kitchen who was passionate about abstract ceramics and had a vague affiliation with Columbia University. She had huge silicone fake tits and a drawn-on mole that punctuated her face, which I thought indicated her talent for knowing what was missing.

You are like ugly duckling, she said. *My* ugly duckling. One day, you swim.

So things were going really well for me when Simon, our landlord, pounded on our door at the end of summer. I opened it. I fucking hated Simon. He wore this bright blue polo tee tight to his biceps and rubbed a hand over his bald head. His parents had left him newly in charge of the building, but he rarely responded to service requests about leaks and broken dryers.

We need to talk, he said.

I stepped outside.

No more late rent.

Got it.

Also, rent is increasing by 30 percent, he said. And *also*, he was in touch with new prospective tenants who were thrilled about his new listings, dirt cheap considering the location (which, for many years now, was incredibly desirable). I didn't know you'd posted the place, I said. I spoke with some interested creatives, he said. Renters' rights? I asked. I could try, he explained, it was well within my rights to try, but this kind of thing was perfectly legal on his part, as the increase would begin with the new lease, which he was writing up now. The old one was about to end, something my dad hadn't told me. There hadn't been a price increase in about ten years, because Simon hadn't been in charge, his dad had, and he'd liked my dad.

I feel this is reasonable, he said then. I understand how hard it's been for you. I *admire* you in fact, taking care of Michael and everything.

He was so condescending.

Also, have you seen Maura?

Of course I had.

No, I said.

She hasn't paid rent in two months.

That's awful, I said. So crazy.

Maura was this leathery, sixty-year-old ex-hippie who was from South Slope but always talked about how she lived for years on the West Coast. She'd gotten on the FREE LAND bus in 1970, in hopes of grabbing free property. The FREE LAND bus was a bus with FREE LAND written on the side. She'd been a screenwriter on a sitcom back in the day, she'd claimed, though she hadn't said which. She had a huge tattoo of a hydrangea on her right bicep, and definitely didn't own land. *Could you hide this?* she'd asked me yesterday, and handed me a sealed manilla envelope. I liked Maura and her secrets. I liked the idea of free land, and of someone hating Simon as much as I do.

Well, let me know if you see her, he said.

Mmhm.

It seemed like we might have to move, or at least have to cancel our vacation. How to break any of that to Michael was a problem.

We'd already decided we'd go to SeaWorld for his birthday in two weeks. It was an average hotel, three stars, but it was his favorite and the only place away from home Michael would ever agree to stay overnight. We used to drive down there, to Orlando, with our dad. There was a swimming pool shaped like a stingray, an LED mushroom fountain that gushed neon water and doubled as a karaoke machine. Occasionally, they hosted banquet hall conferences for bondage furries or ex-cops, or people who all owned dachshunds.

I didn't like un-promising things, and in all honesty, I wanted to go too.

*   *   *

My sculptures lately were ceramic rocks and cups made to look like rock, sometimes frosted or crumpled, like stuff I'd find walking along local beaches, the edges of broken glass, the texture of shells. In a gallery space, I'd collect them and incorporate running water, which Kitty Kitchen board members approved of, though the idea was only sketched out so far.

Michael liked to sculpt too. I'd lay out tarps in the living room and he'd sculpt self-portraits from gray clay over and over, always his head, always busts of different sizes. For two eyes, he used plastic peel-away gemstones. All his heads were lined up along the kitchen counter, gemstone eyes staring straight ahead. He liked to watch South Park while he sculpted, and would pace around squeaking, copying the obscenities. He drank crispy Diet Coke with crushed ice. Lately, he was obsessed with crushed ice and the idea of the SeaWorld ice cream man, the one who'd sold us blueberry soft serve out of a cart at the theme park when we were kids. Blueberry soft serve was hard to come by; in fact, it kind of seemed like it didn't exist outside of SeaWorld. Back then it was always the same man, every summer.

Are we gonna see him? Michael asked me again, pressing his two fingers into the clay to make eyes. The man?

Michael resisted change most of all and wanted everything to stay the same forever and ever. I wasn't allowed, for example, to use the word "beard," in reference to the hair that sometimes showed up on his chin, because he didn't want to grow up. I wasn't allowed to say his real age either. So, I just silently bought him razors and handed them over, and he took care of it.

We have to wait and see about the ice cream man, I said. Like, he might've retired. He's ultimately just some guy.

I *know* that, he said. I just like to think about him.

We cleaned up and walked across the street and down past brownstones and the fenced edge of the overpass. From there you could see the Statue of Liberty, which Michael pointed out each time without fail.

There she is, he said. He held his hand up to his forehead like a pioneer.

Should we go to Trader Joe's? I asked.

I just don't feel like it today. Okay?

No problem.

We passed a garden of bougainvillea. A monarch fluttered past his face and he flinched. He had a fear of butterflies—I swatted it away. Something about the brisk, unpredictable quality of movement.

Past that was the deli. Stan waved. Friend of our dad's. Next door, we saw a brand new coffee shop, where Ed's used to be. It seemed like just last week Ed's was still there. My dad too.

It's different, he said, processing the change. Ed's is gone, he said, then turned to observe whether I understood too.

Ed's was this horrible pizza shop, decades old. We'd order baked garlic bread knots sometimes, however shitty they were. Ed's wife cut hair in the area too, not mine since high school, but still. We loved Ed's.

Instead of Ed's peeling painted white facade, the cafe facade was now gray black and featureless. Out front, a square wrought iron sign hung over the door: Three Sparrows.

Can we go in there? he said, curious now.

I guess.

I'm gonna go in myself, okay? he said, as in, *don't follow me, please.*

Got it, I said, sitting at the table out front. You want money?

No, I have money, he said. Michael saved his monthly government stipend, which he got for being autistic. He held onto about two thousand dollars in his piggy bank at any given point, which, I sometimes considered, was insane. It was a lot of money.

He went inside and came back holding a muffin.

How much?

Actually none, he said. I didn't have to pay. He sat and unwrapped his muffin, peeling the crimped parchment away.

Why not?

He shrugged. Don't know.

She said it was free?!

I don't know, *okay?* She just said I didn't have to pay. He bit the baked blueberry-thick edge.

I felt vaguely concerned that he'd misunderstood, but that was unlike him. He understood rules, and in fact thrived knowing exactly the limits prescribed, in all situations, which I considered one of his best qualities. The clay has to dry before we paint it, he'd say to himself. He had strong concepts, which he knew how to commit to. Once, when he was mad at me for being late to pick him up from school, I came home to find a trail of sticky notes leading from the front door, through the hall, to the bathroom. In the bathroom he lay on his back playing dead, with one big sticky note stuck to his chest: LAST KID.

I got up and walked inside. The woman at the register wore white overalls. She was serving a woman with a dog on one leash and a little kid on the other. She smiled at me, then carefully carried her matcha away.

Hi, the barista said. He's the sweetest! She smiled an inarguably pretty smile, even if self-satisfied. An Anne Hathaway smile, fake humble with maybe-Veneers. Are you his aide?

Oh no, he's my brother. But thank you, I said. And thank you for the muffin.

Oh! I see. Her face brightened. Embarrassed, maybe. Why? No reason to be. Uncomfortable? I didn't mind that. Michael and I had pushed past shame, for instance, over his disability, and didn't easily succumb to discomfort. But weirdly I felt a small thrill. I sort of liked seeing someone else uncomfortable for a change, caught off guard.

She just sort of smiled. Well, *love* that, she said. He's the cutest. He offered to tip. So good with his words too, she continued. Very articulate.

He could be bad with his words sometimes, actually, especially with strangers. This of course bothered me, as in, sometimes what I knew he wanted to convey was not conveyed to others. Of course that bothered me; it would bother anyone. It bothered me that sometimes we couldn't even share the same thoughts or words, or that I wasn't always sure which ones we did share.

But the fact that she'd clocked this trait wasn't what made me dislike her, even if it made me feel vulnerable, like she'd seen something intimate of Michael, of me. I just didn't particularly like that she'd called him "cute."

I'd like to pay, I said. Could I just go ahead and pay for it?

Oh. Okay sure. She blinked at me. She hadn't actually said anything wrong, I just didn't like her. She was around my age, a few years out of college. I felt her staring at my face, the way someone does when they figure they could know you outside of the given circumstance. And "cute." Kind of bold. *Presumptuous.* I felt the need to shield him, the wrong impulse to have. Like I couldn't trust others with him, of course they'd act weird.

What's his name? she asked.

Michael.

What's your name?

Sasha.

Nice to meet you. I'm Mackenzie, she said. We're new, still getting to know the area. Really loving it so far.

Yeah, I see. I handed her ten dollars.

She took it and gave me a terse smile. Well, he's the sweetest. She held the bills up as if to say *thanks.* So polite.

It was true, he'd been raised polite.

Mackenzie continued to stare at me. I actually thought maybe she liked me. Really, really liked me. I felt a strange surge of something teenage in me. I hated this girl.

Have a good rest of your day, I said.

* * *

Lucas sat on my couch and rambled. Our fascination with aliens is fucking nuts, he said. There are aliens *all* around us.

He showed me a video on his phone of big killer whales like Shamu, carving through water colored artificially blue, in a massive aquarium. They bleated at each other, communicating like we do, the best ways to trap their prey, and balletically, they go right, go left, circle, and now, eat.

The whale drifted like a balloon, fins outstretched.

He's big, Michael said.

Lucas, my best friend, was over at ours scouring the internet for jobs on his laptop. Recently, he'd been paid to participate in a study in which he attached electrodes to his brain and then watched Pornhub for an hour. Lucas never seemed uncomfortable about the things I would've been uncomfortable about, things that should have been private. Lucas made a point of trying to diminish his shame; it was often how he made his money.

Do you have any food? he asked, now, rifling through my fridge. I'm starving.

I'm not sure, I said. We went to this cafe today. Three Sparrows. Have you been there?

No.

It's brand new, I said.

Oh okay. Why?

The barista was rude to Michael, I said.

What did they say?!

I don't know. She gave him a free blueberry muffin and told him he didn't have to pay.

Lucas blinked. That seems nice?

I shrugged. She probably felt pretty good, giving a muffin to the autistic teenager, I thought. That wasn't even what annoyed me. She could have that. I just didn't like her, or her smooth face. I imagined the smooth heads of her delicious buttermilk blueberry muffins, smooth all over.

Lucas mindlessly typed Three Sparrows into his phone. Michael entered the living room and watched as we scrolled through the Yelp reviews.

There was a picture of eggs benedict and a selfie of a woman, the camera very close to her face. **Yummy!!! I LOVE. Heart eye emoji.**

Another picture of a teenage girl with a muffin, holding up a peace sign. **So good love this spot. And owner Mackenzie is so sweet!**

She's the owner, I said.

Lucas was obviously kind of bored. He glanced back at his laptop.

God. Fuck these people. My dad would've *hated* to see this, I said. I imagined my dad saying: *The neighborhood is going to SHIT. GODDAMMIT.* And slamming a Michelob Ultra.

I know, Lucas said. He'd heard me say it a thousand times before. But that is what happens, he said. People move to New York. People always will. It's the number one place people move. You can't be in constant agony over it.

I nodded.

I don't know, it could be worse. Simon could be tripling the rent? You had it pretty good for a while.

Still, I said.

I hear you. Maybe you should leave a bad Yelp review, he said, and was kidding.

Maybe I will, I said, taking his phone. I scrolled more. Mackenzie's picture again.

She has a pig nose, Michael said. He stood near us now.

Write that, Lucas said.

Haha, Michael said. Pig nose. He did the pig nose at Lucas.

Pig, I wrote.

I typed out the rest of it, then showed it to Lucas. He kind of laughed, and then also typed a line or two. He handed it back to me.

Is this really mean? I asked.

Lucas stared at me for a second. Yes, he said. I mean, that will probably upset her.

Maybe it'll keep people away, I said.

I went to hit post.

Wait, you can't.

Why not?

He stared at me like I was dumb. It's a terrorist threat, he said. But also, he was amused. Come on. Don't actually post it.

I shrugged. Doesn't have my name on it. Instead of listening, I made a Google account with a nonsensical password and posted it.

Don't come to the cafe tomorrow. I was there on Friday and owner Mackenzie kicked out a homeless teenager who asked for water. She was literally on the verge of tears. How fucking hard is it to give out water?? What a pig. Neighborhood is going to shit and I for one am sick and tired.

This is a warning. Everyone gets what they deserve.

*   *   *

On our walk the next day we passed the cafe again. The facade was black and featureless as the Pornhub website. Mackenzie was there. She waved, with a sort of half-smile. I waved back, then realized Michael was already walking inside again. I assumed she hadn't seen the Yelp review, which all in all, was ridiculously written. There was no way any person would take it seriously.

I know you, she said to Michael, in a sort of cute way. Muffin?

He nodded, smiled. Blueberry please.

I felt sudden guilt then, seeing how comfortable he seemed. Maybe she was nice. What was wrong with me?

Thank you, Michael said. Appreciate it.

He *was* raised polite.

She gave Michael a blueberry muffin for free, as if to say: I am standing my ground, please take the free muffin, I insist. Thanks, Michael said, taking his muffin with two careful hands. He looked to me. Should I–?

Yes, I confirmed. Go ahead and pay.

Would you actually want to pay? he said, in a sneaky way.

Sure. Go sit.

He was pleased at this.

How's your day? she asked.

I blinked at her. No malice in her voice at all. She must not have read the review. In a way, I was grateful she hadn't. Or, she had read it and was putting up a good front. If she had read it, how could she know it was me? That was ridiculous. I was just standing there with Michael, who had a way of disarming people. He was charming. "Cute."

I pointed to a row of ceramics near the espresso beans. That's nice, I said, lying.

I sell them, she said, proudly. My girlfriend's.

Gay, I considered. Interesting. I tapped a small ceramic jewelry tray, priced seventy-five dollars by sticky note. Nothing of note about it. A subtle glaze. Identity deficient, featureless. I'd have bet she wielded her gayness as much as she could, however featurelessly. What about Ed, who'd always made an honest living? I knew what an honest living was, I liked to tell myself. I told myself a lot, but nothing really stuck. Stuff went into my head and out of it. I never understood what the right thing was. I just knew what I'd heard and what I'd told myself. Sometimes this scared me.

I make ceramics too, I said, slightly defeated.

Oh! she said, smiling, delighted. You know, we sell other peoples' crafts—people who live in the neighborhood. We're having an art party pretty soon!

Crafts, I thought. Knickknacks. I'm on a *fellowship,* I wanted to say, and the impulse disturbed me. There was a set of polymer clay ketchup bottle earrings on a rack nearby.

I'm actually doing a fellowship, I said, in spite of myself. For ceramics.

Oh, no way. So is my girlfriend.

Nice.

Yeah! It's the Kitty Kitchen fellowship. For ceramics. She's really loving it, so far.

*   *   *

Later that day, we walked around the corner to the rec center to swim. It was humid-hot even though it was September. My skin was sticky and I felt tired.

Michael looked down at his green crocs, kicked at a pile of broken concrete. I like his hat the most, he explained. I like his hat because it covers his eyebrows, so he doesn't look mean.

He'd been fixated on eyebrows for a few years now. If a person's eyebrows were severe—tattooed or drawn-on—he often perceived them as mean, evil even.

I get what you're saying, but remember what *I* said.

I know. Eyebrows don't mean you're evil.

No, about the man, I said. We have to wait and see.

What is the ice cream man's hat called? His hat covers his eyebrows.

I'm not sure.

At the rec center swimming pool, I sat on the plain white lawn chair with my legs up and crossed, hoping the UV index might be somehow enough to tan me even though it was nearly fall. I lay there and thought about the ceramic jewelry tray. It's just a jewelry tray, I reminded myself. Nothing wrong with it, just a jewelry tray.

Don't look, Michael said, urgently.

Huh? I said, on edge.

There's a bee. I listened with my eyes closed as he slipped out of the water, sloshing wet, and padded over to where I was and squashed the bee dead. Michael always killed the bugs for me. I hated bugs. He never minded. His only phobia was butterflies.

Don't be scared, he said. That's nonsense. He said nonsense like he'd heard it on TV. That's *nonsense.*

Maura walked through the gate. I waved for her to come over, lowered my sunglasses.

Simon's looking for you, I said.

God, she said.

Simon's a retard, Michael said, swishing around in the water. He slapped a hand into the water. I'm gonna kill him.

Today, I didn't scold him for saying that. Sometimes I let him have fun.

Simon is just *SO* rude! Maura shouted.

I shielded my eyes. Maura, do you drink coffee?

No honey. Hi Michael.

Maura, remember you told me about the free land bus? I said.

Free land? Oh! Sure. Yes.

Did you ever get the land?

Oh no. No no. But I did live with some Natives for a while. My first husband was Cherokee. She turned to Michael. You like the pool? Can I come in too?

Sure, Michael said. Come in. He leaned back and dunked his head in, then went blurry under the surface. I wanted badly as always to communicate exactly what I thought: that it was hard to see the neighborhood change, that I was scared. That there was more than a neighborhood out there, there was an actual world. He knew that, sort of, and sometimes sensed he wasn't part of it. I'm autistic, he'd observe sometimes. That's why I'm scared of eyebrows, as in, I'm scared of other people, their expressions, what they mean when they talk. He had great instincts. But still, he didn't always know the full extent of what he was missing.

Maura slipped off her pants to reveal her one-piece. Then she backstroked toward the other end of the pool.

That woman at the new coffee shop is awful, I told Maura. Just warning you.

I don't drink coffee, honey. She dipped beneath the surface.

Who are you talking about? he asked.

Mackenzie, I said. I think she's *mean*, I clarified. I don't want to go to that place anymore, I told him. Bottom line.

She's nice to me. She gives me free food. Why mean?

I felt badly, then. "Mean" wasn't correct.

Mackenzie does have a funny face, he said, after some thought. She has weird eyebrows. In South Park Cartman doesn't always have eyebrows.

No, I said, solemnly.

Michael covered both his eyebrows with his hands. No eyebrows, he said, and glanced up at mine. Are we gonna see the ice cream man at SeaWorld? he asked.

Yeah, I hope so.

He lowered his hands. I feel like, in my head, he's always there though, he said, trying to make me understand. It will feel weird if he's not. It just won't be the same without him.

*   *   *

The next day, Michael, Lucas, and I walked past Three Sparrows. Huge on the front door was a poster with Mackenzie's face.

Missing:
Mackenzie Lowell
Please share. Last seen wearing
orange beanie, hiking shoes.

When she smiled, a little too much gum showed. Her mousy brown hair looked tousled in the wind. In this image she looked like anybody. She looked like an AI rendering of a missing child grown up, her skin soft with an optimistic glow. She *was* mousy, derogatorily. Brunette. The kind of person that blends into a crowd. It frightened me that this girl could be anywhere.

My stomach turned. That's the woman, I said.

Lucas blinked, looked more closely. The one who gave you guys free muffins?

Some other woman picked up her dog, walked to look at the poster. Concern grew on her face.

Who's working inside? I asked, urgently.

Uhhh some guy. Mustache. Big glasses.

I stared at Lucas. So she's missing?

Lucas stared back, at a loss.

What? Michael said, sensing panic. Is everything okay?

I jogged inside.

Hey, I said. I stood next to the college-aged boy ordering, startling him. What happened to Mackenzie?

The male barista had long curly hair. He was steaming almond milk. He cleared his throat, glanced around, like it was a sensitive topic.

They don't know, he said. He shook his head solemnly, lips a terse line. We're holding out hope.

The row of blueberry muffins sat in the case, fresh baked, uneaten.

Do they know anything at all?

He shrugged, glanced around again. Not yet. It's rattled everybody, he said, in a low voice. Her family too. It's just such horrible timing. She just opened up the place. Worked really hard to do it. Things were going well. It's disheartening.

He stared at the ground for a minute, then back up at me. What's your name?

Sasha.

Collin. Nice to meet you. He stuck his hand out to shake. Come in anytime. Even if you just want to talk. He was immediately friendly, forthcoming in a way that seemed inherently false, though he himself didn't seem to know it was.

I know it's been hard on everybody, he said, nodding.

And then, I swore, I thought he might be tearing up.

*   *   *

Lucas and I just sat next to each other on my couch that night, drinking. The Snoopy Thanksgiving special came on the TV, so early in the year. It was September but the months were pushing onward, quickly.

Do you think somebody killed her? I said.

Calm down, Lucas said, setting his glass down on my table, no coaster. No, I really don't. I think it's a coincidence and I think you need to stop thinking about it.

He seemed unbothered about it. Or maybe, just pretending to be unbothered, watching Snoopy intently.

I stared at Snoopy in his chef's hat, heating popcorn up on the stove. It popped and flew. How can you be so sure? I said, trying to seem levelheaded.

Because it was a harmless stupid post. There's just no way it mattered that much.

I leaned forward and put my head in my hands. Where do you think her girlfriend is, in all this? She said she had a girlfriend.

Lucas shrugged.

On the TV was the Snoopy scene where he fights a folding chair that he can't get to open. It keeps snapping shut. Eventually, the chair gets sick of Snoopy trying to pry it open and comes to life, with fists, and after much antagonizing, they beat each other up.

Shouldn't we take the post down then? I said.

Do you remember the username or password? Didn't you use a fake account?

I can't just sit here, I said. I need to *do* something.

Let's take a walk.

So we walked silently down the street to an Irish bar we liked, just us two. Michael was fast asleep. The drinks were dirt cheap and the owner played Irish ballads during Happy Hour, wailing along sadly, mournfully.

We didn't make her disappear, did we? I said, a few hours later, with severity, with too much spiritual gravity. I was the kind of drunk where I'd start talking about ghosts or God and I could sense, then, that I'd already asked Lucas that same thing quite a few times, but couldn't stop myself from asking. My speech slipped out and away, hovering apart from me.

You did this, Lucas said, finally. *I* didn't do anything.

You let me post it.

He seemed unhappy.

I checked Yelp, squinting at my phone in the dark bar, which seemed too bright. Our post was gone. Removed, I guessed, due to violating community guidelines.

I showed Lucas, then pocketed my phone, ordered another mezcal soda.

Maybe a cider or something instead, Lucas said.

To me, it seemed like a good thing it was gone. Our problem was erased, scrubbed away. If nobody could read it, it couldn't cause any damage. Some dumb lapse in judgment.

I'll get the next drink, Lucas sighed. It's on me, he said, softening.

What if someone saw the post and *killed* her? I asked. Like found her and got rid of her? Took care of her?

Lucas glanced around like I'd said it too loudly. I don't think that's the case, he said, again, trying to curtail my wildest guesses, even though I would continue to ruminate, and continue to make him curtail.

The only semblance of autism in me was maybe my inability to discriminate as far as what people, what Lucas especially, knew about me. He had to know everything. I had to disclose everything or else I'd be lying. I had to get everything in, however difficult or inconvenient. Lucas knew about all of my problems. How can you know me if I don't spread it all out for you to see clearly? I had to talk things over and over, too, over and over to death so I knew, for sure, what the answer was, until the thing itself was sufficiently studied, tiresome enough to be shoved from my head. I couldn't risk reaching the wrong answer. So I obsessed.

Two months before, I'd drunkenly led Lucas to a house party bathroom and said: just do it already. Do what? he'd asked. Just do whatever you want to me. What does *that* mean? he said, startled. You *know* what it means, I'd said. You won't, I'd said, spitefully, so full of spite I scared myself, thinking back on it afterwards. Why haven't you done it yet? I'd said. You know what I'm talking about. And he wouldn't kiss me. Not now, he said. So he saw what I maybe might've wanted, what I thought he wanted too. He had to know everything.

He walked me back home tonight. For the first time, I felt maybe he was mad at me, for all of it.

*　*　*

I woke up with a pounding headache. I made myself useful and pushed the couch aside and vacuumed, then swiped the kitchen counter.

Michael had placed his piggy bank on the kitchen counter. I lifted it to clean. That's one thing my dad never did: smash Michael's bank open and use the insides. That would have been near impossible to explain to Michael, the violence toward the piggy bank, whose name was Oliver. There'd be hell to pay if he were crushed to pink ceramic.

I'll be taking that, Michael said, and lifted Oliver. That's mine, thanks, he said, and tucked him under his arm. You okay? He could tell something was off.

I'm fine, I said. All good.

He showed me Oliver, whose one eyebrow lifted quizzically, as if knowing some secret. I tapped his head.

I took extra shifts at the Venetian-Italian restaurant. I started a new project proposal draft for Kitty Kitchen. On Instagram, Three Sparrows posted the flyer for Mackenzie's disappearance. Last seen, it explained, taking the PATH train to New Jersey. The most recent post was a flyer advertising the communal art show Mackenzie had described. Free drinks. I sent it to Lucas.

As always it seemed to go without saying between us, that of course we'd go.

*   *   *

We went to the art party a week later, which served cold brew and alcohol at the same time. Local artists, like Mackenzie had promised, had contributed to the party, but no Mackenzie. "In her name," I thought I heard someone say, like she was dead. I wondered if they'd channel funds toward search efforts.

Lucas and I browsed the art for sale. It was a random mix. There were air-brushed floral motifs on a big drape-y canvas, air-brushed bees buzzing around it. Multicolored Navajo friendship bracelets. Ultra-realistic charcoal portraits of different dead rappers. Intimate oil paintings of the same teenage girl in vaguely compromising poses: legs spread while licking an ice cream cone. The girl who'd clearly drawn them was sitting next to them, sipping a hot chocolate. I thought I recognized her from the pool. Wedged between the artists' booths, I worried I shouldn't have come.

Lucas picked up a friendship bracelet the color of pea soup. Mine was yellow like cartoon sunshine.

Modest amounts of champagne in plastic flutes sat in a row on the stained wood countertop. Lucas and I downed several.

Eventually, we were greeted by Collin, the emotional barista I'd met earlier.

Hey, this is Lane, Collin said. She runs a gallery in the area.

Lane was beautiful, with long black hair. She wore these vintage black-heeled boots.

Oh great, Lucas said, casually. Lucas seemed miserable, in general, to be there. Had I dragged him here? He'd agreed, I'd thought.

I live in the building down the block, I said. The pale yellow one.

Oh, Simon, of course, Lane said. I know him. He owns most of the buildings on that block, right?

Owns, I thought. Taking credit for what his family does. I had this dull bitter feeling, something I was beholden to but already bored of.

I think I've seen you guys around. You and your…?

Brother. Michael, I said.

Then, I couldn't stop myself.

I'm a sculptor, I said. Focusing on ceramics right now.

Ohh cool.

I started describing my work to Lane, who nodded, smiled politely.

That's awesome, she said. And, must be nice to live in one of Simon's buildings. They're a steal, and so beautiful. Historic inside.

Simon's a great guy.

Lane nodded vigorously.

But to be honest, he put my neighbor out on the street last week, I lied. Did you hear about that?

Lane was uncomfortable then. Wow, *no*, I didn't know that. A hesitation showed on her face, a resistance, a skepticism.

It's been… a challenge. It's been challenging, I would say, and I looked to Lucas for reassurance. He didn't meet my gaze. It's been a challenge for Michael and me.

Lane seemed intrigued, then, interested in the subversion of her idea of Simon, in my blatant disapproval. That's just awful, she said. Wow wow, I had no idea. Wow.

Simon, I said, and closed my eyes, and thought, *don't say it.* Simon complained about Michael too, I said. Complained about the noise. It's just hard, you know, when people don't understand Michael. It can be pretty hard.

She looked at me like she cared, then. I would've said anything, in that moment, to make her care even more. I could've said anything at all. It was so easy to just say anything I wanted, to have that care.

Lucas downed champagne, miserably. I could tell he was hoping I would shut the fuck up, confused at how I hadn't shut the fuck up already. I fell out of my drunkenness. My face got hot. Lucas hating me, I couldn't handle. Lucas not being on my side.

That's… *awful,* Lane whispered. God.

*   *   *

Lucas and I were on our way out when we saw Ed.

Sasha! Oh boy. How's everything? Ed seemed jovial, red-faced. He held a half-full champagne flute, and wore his same khaki slacks and crisp white t-shirt.

Ed, what happened? I said. I went to hug him. Too personal, probably, but he loved it. Michael and I miss the garlic bread, I said. His hug was warm, familiar.

I sold the place! he said. Made great money.

To Mackenzie?

Yeah. Heartbreaking, what's going on with her.

But don't you think a place like this is kind of… bad?

Lucas kicked at a square of sidewalk that had chipped away from the ground, revealing a dark square.

Ed shrugged. Bad how? People love this place!

Well. Just different.

She made me a rich man, I'll tell you that much, he said. Finally, I can retire. After twenty-five GODDAMN years. Your dad would be happy to know *that.* God*damn.*

Someone touched my back. Lane. She handed me her card. If you have a website, send it over. Sooo nice to meet you.

She smelled amazing. Whatever perfume she had on smelled like wet leaves and lilac. She clacked away in her Prada boots, toward the train.

Why do you keep lying to people? What the fuck is wrong with you? Lucas said.

We started walking towards home.

What do you mean?

You keep making everything worse. It's like you can't stop making everything worse.

What does it matter? Everything's already *worse*.

He stopped and rubbed at his face. I'm gonna go home. I have to be up early.

Why?

You're acting pathetic and I don't want any part of it. I'm tired of you making me part of it. I'm tired of you complaining and then lying even more for attention. Nobody *did* anything to you. *You're* digging your own hole.

He left me there alone.

*   *   *

I came home visibly distraught, visibly drunk. I lay down flat on the couch, my arms stretched back.

What's wrong? Michael asked. He stood in the hallway entry.

We can't go to SeaWorld, I said, finally. I sat up.

He looked startled at the severity of the comment. *Why?*

There's not enough money.

He ran his fingertips down the door frame, thinking. I have money, he said.

No.

But I have Oliver.

No.

Why not?

Because we'd have to break him, I said.

He stared at me. Yes we can, he said. That's what Oliver is for.

We'd have to take a hammer and smash him into pieces.

He considered this. We have to break him to go to SeaWorld?

Yeah.

Let's break him then. Haha. With a hammer?

Are you sure? That's your money, I said.

Yeah sounds fun. Let's break him. He's gonna yell like this: AHHHH.

Exactly.

He considered the destruction of Oliver. Then, he seemed upset, actually. Why didn't you ask me? he said. Why didn't you ask of course?

I don't know.

That's silly. You always know. If something goes wrong, we ask for money, he said, like it was an old saying. Just like if you go to jail, you ask for help.

That's true.

Am I gonna go to jail? he said. Can they take you to jail for clowning around?

No Michael. I'm sorry I didn't ask.

Can we break him now?

Let's do it tomorrow.

Okay fine. He rubbed his eye, tired, now. Next time, just ask. That's nonsense. Of course there's money.

Guilt washed across me. I hadn't realized how much I'd failed to explain, not even trying for fear he wouldn't get it.

Next time, I'll ask, I said. Promise.

*   *   *

Early the next morning, Lucas texted me. My hangover felt like wearing a helmet, like a headache tightly fitted to my head. He was probably mad at me. I would apologize. As always. I rolled over in bed.

Instead, he'd texted: *You need to see this.* And attached an article.

Cafe owner Mackenzie Lowell found dead in an abandoned swimming pool in New Jersey.

Michael could tell, by my face, that something was wrong, when I walked to the kitchen counter, started mindlessly making coffee.

Are you sad? he said.

No, I said.

I wished, hard, that I could explain. I was so hungover that the idea of trying seemed completely out of reach. How would I start? "I should not have posted to Yelp."

He left the room, then retrieved Oliver. He placed Oliver on the counter. Here he is. Like I said. Okay? So we can use him. Okay?

I nodded. Okay. Thank you. That's perfect.

I could tell, now, that he was remembering our dad, and sadness, seeing me sad, and remembering how unprepared we'd been, how sudden his death was: an unforeseen heart attack so silent and so quick, one day here, one day gone.

Everything's okay, I said. We're going to SeaWorld!

He nodded. He took the information in, processed it, paused. Can I watch South Park?

Of course.

I read on. There was foul play suspected. Allegedly, she'd been intoxicated at the time, and found all alone. An investigation was underway. No security footage. At the end of the article, they prompted the public to come forward with any leads they had, which implied they didn't have very many. I wondered if it was possible they'd find my archived post. Even if deleted, surely it could be found.

In my room, I sat at my desk. I sculpted a pitted swimming pool shape, asymmetrical like a kidney bean, but also rounded, with a cavernous, hollowed bottom, kind of like a half-shell.

I molded clay with my hands. I didn't normally make figurative stuff but this time, I made a tiny girl, sitting on the edge of the pool. I attached a tiny arm to her abdomen. She had a peanut head and her tits were globs. She was rudimentary. I squashed her, embarrassed that I'd tried. I balled her up.

I walked out to the living room, the carpet fresh with vacuum tracks. Michael had turned South Park on. Cartman wore no clothes, his bright white body doughy, no penis visible. His squeaking sounded sort of buried, but comforting, under the AC on full blast.

If Michael and I couldn't live here, on our own terms, forever, I didn't want to live anywhere. She was worth that.

Michael lounged on the couch. Can we have blueberry muffins? He asked.

I worked my shift later that day, in silence at the Venetian-Italian tavern. I swiped a rag across the same tables over and over again.

Lucas came in.

Are you mad at me? I asked. I'm really sorry. I don't really know what I'm doing sometimes.

No, he said. I just don't want to think about Mackenzie anymore. I want to move on. He said it like it was for both of us.

I'm sorry I said it was your fault, I said.

He shrugged. I'm used to it. Then he kind of smiled. The sky seemed fake blue. It was perfect vacation weather.

Do you think we killed her? He asked. Do you really think that?

I shrugged. You definitely didn't, I said.

You didn't either, he said. He knocked my arm, like usual, and I liked the thought of continuing, just the same as usual. He sat at the bar. An Aperol spritz, *please?*

It was that my lies felt like the truth, that's why I'd told them. I held what Lucas said in my head, that it wasn't me who'd hurt anyone, it couldn't have possibly been me, saying something out loud didn't just make it come true. I wanted so badly to believe him.

We never talked about her again.

*   *   *

My alarm went off as planned at 4am. Michael had been up since even earlier.

He parted my blinds for me, then ran a hand across them like they were wind chimes. They made a paper-clatter. He whispered, Wake up Sasha. SeaWorld.

He stood in his boxers but also wearing his SeaWorld visor, embroidered with the outlines of dolphins. He looked like what you picture when you think: that's a young man. You look bad, he said. You okay?

Just early, I said. I threw the covers off. Let's go.

I hauled canvas grocery bags of random things out to our car. Our apartment complex stood fading yellow in the early sun.

Can we bring this? Michael said. It was a DVD boxset of every single South Park episode from 2005 to 2010.

I leaned against the car, sweating. No. We're not gonna have time to watch it, I said. We'll be at SeaWorld.

But could I just bring one?

I'm not sure that makes sense, I told him.

He agreed. We don't need it.

In the car, we sped across the bridge. I lost visibility for the few seconds it took to enter the Holland Tunnel, a sudden dark cast across the windshield, the tunnel too dark against the bright day. I hit the gas and could see again, everything lit up yellow.

Michael loved tunnels. He rolled both his windows down. Yellow light bulbs everywhere, light flicking past.

I rolled my window down too. I chose not to feel guilt. I wouldn't even think of her. In my rearview, Michael was happy.

I'm thinking about the ice cream man's eyebrows, Michael said. I want to think about them forever.

Please let him be there, I thought.

*   *   *

We drove for hours, no stops. I wanted to drive the whole way straight through. Michael slept. Eventually the ocean appeared, the gulls screeching. We arrived at his favorite hotel, which looked exactly as it had, six years ago when we'd last been there. We dropped our stuff off, smeared sunscreen on our faces, and headed straight for the theme park.

The ice cream man, Michael said, once again. But he was happier now, anticipatory.

We have to wait and see, I said, but felt eager then too.

I know. You always say that.

We entered the park. A huge blue waterslide towered in the distance. I felt the kid-thrill of being at an amusement park. We passed the gift shop, saw the charms and seashells coated in glitter paint, and walked immediately to the dolphin tank, which was massive. When the cold air hit, it revived me. The charge of dolphins together in their small rocky grotto, bleating with their tiny teeth and perpetual smiles.

Two killer whales, water-slick and black, heaved their heavy bodies up and out of the water, whales so powerful they could literally kill with one clean pound downward. I remembered standing there as kids, when it felt like there was more to glean about the world, like this break in our normalcy was opportunity, like there was understanding I suddenly had access to. We liked to be pressed up against the glass, looking closely at the same thing.

Now before I could stop him, Michael slipped from reach, and ran. Quickly I turned to see where. He ran hard toward the ice cream man with his cart, and it was the same guy, just grayer in the hair, with his same white cap. I held my breath as he charged, faster than I'd ever seen him run.

I ran after him. I felt the sudden surge of power you feel as a kid racing another kid, when you near the end of the track and there's only so much time to close the gap. I ran until the cement turned to grass and the ice cream man came into view. His hat! I heard Michael shout, not just to himself, but to me. I saw the ice cream man wave. Michael waved back. I ran to catch up.

AURORA HUIZA is a New-York based writer originally from Los Angeles. Her writing has appeared online at Expat Press, X-R-A-Y, Rejection Letters, *and others. She is a recent graduate of the Syracuse MFA Program for fiction. Her X is @ aurora_huiza_.*

Disfigured: An Essay

Emilie Pascale Beck

The dog seemed old from the time we got him, as if he was acting the part of an elderly man. At the shelter, they said probably two. The vet said likely four. This makes him, now, either sixteen or eighteen. He's nearly blind and mostly deaf. Also, he's got arthritis in his back legs, as well as a cough that's due partially to an enlarged heart and partially to a collapsing trachea—a grotesque sound, somewhere between a honking goose and wet choking. He's had epilepsy since we adopted him, which is controlled by a bucketful of daily medications. There's a growth on his right hip, which he worries with his tongue and teeth. It looks like a wad of bubble gum that someone chewed and stuck on him: gruesome but benign. I tape a large bandage over it that ends up being even more of an invitation for him to rip it off, eat it, then lick the growth until it bleeds.

Ha ha, I imagine the dog saying in the voice that Jack and I pretend for him. *Not dead yet.*

It's wet outside this morning when he needs to be let out. From the back deck to the ground are three stairs. Stepping onto the first, he slips, rolls over, tumbles down the other two and rights himself before I can move. Afterward, he seems unhurt though disoriented.

I guide him toward the section that we leave to him, underneath the plum tree, then back to the house when he's done. Not wanting a repeat of his fall, I carry him up the stairs, despite what it will cost me.

Every day, we say that it's a wonder he's alive.

*   *   *

I wore, during my teenage years, a white, plastic back brace—like a corset—for scoliosis. My crooked spine was discovered at age ten. In recent years, the curvature has suddenly doubled. One side of my back has become tightly compressed. My pelvis now rotates to the right as if lagging behind the rest of my body. From the outside, hardly noticeable, but at my annual wellness exam the nurse measured me two inches shorter from one year to the next. This was one of the first signs that it was getting worse. Also: the pain.

The way I can understand how much pain I'm in now is to remember that I once was not at all. I did things that caused temporary aches, but they had nothing on this current, unrelenting level of torment. (Is *torment* too strong of a word? Would *agony* be better?) If it does recede, it's only to the edges, where it returns with any misstep. Doctors ask me when it's most intense. *Walking,* I tell them. *Sitting. Standing. Sleeping.* I hear how it sounds.

*   *   *

When Jack and I first moved into this house, a huge avocado tree towered above the balcony off our bedroom. I'd lean over the railing to pluck the fruit. Green and watery. Fresh. Ours. But only a few years later, the tree became barren. We called arborists who recommended this or that (none of which had any effect), until, finally, one told us that the tree was, in fact, dying. The roots of an avocado tree want to stretch out quite far in all directions, and when they're thwarted—in this case, by the house, the cement path—the tree eventually gives up.

We mourned the loss. Its fruit. Its shade. But out it went because a dead tree is no use to anyone.

*   *   *

I've been going through boxes of old correspondence and diaries. Hundreds, maybe thousands of programs from plays I've attended since I was a child. Dozens of shows I've performed in or directed. It's difficult for me to let go of anything. I worry that I won't remember who I was.

In my early twenties, I was cast in a production that ran first in San Francisco, then in Paris. The *auteur* was an art historian rather than either playwright or director, but I was young and eager, and he was paying my way to France. The piece was autobiographical: years earlier, the *auteur* and his wife had been in a terrible car accident. Only he had survived. This, at first, made him worthy of sympathy. Before rehearsals began, he went to Mexico for a long weekend and contracted hepatitis, both A and B. He began rehearsals wearing a mask, his skin beneath it yellow.

In the cast of four, there was a woman, a pianist, who was attached to her instrument by way of a giant skirt that we laced her into each night. She played Chopin, Rachmaninoff, etc., while a man recited the only spoken words of the evening. My friend Tracy and I played characters called "The Widows," performing acts such as dancing a tango together or playing catch with a large ball that had been hung from the lighting grid. When we had to move from one place to another, we rolled on the floor. We were not to walk, only to roll. Or dance. Mutely.

An acrobat was brought in to instruct me in aerial work. In one segment, I climbed a rope and swung my body upside down, entwining my right leg so the rest of my limbs could be free, my hands above my head—meaning, pointed towards the ground— then I circled, slowly, slowly, all the way down. For the run in California, our stage had some spring to it, but in Paris, it was a hard floor, maybe even cement. I didn't think about asking for any kind of protection or cushioning, so confident was I in my body to perform this trick, which was, once I learned it, relatively easy.

For each performance, the *auteur* sat at the lightboard, which he'd placed in the audience. He sometimes referred to himself as the *improvositeur des lumières.* At any moment onstage, I would find myself in complete darkness, or suddenly in light where I'd previously been hidden. At one point in the *spectacle*, I stood downstage left and slowly, slowly, moved from standing to sitting and then lying down without—ostensibly—the audience seeing me in motion. The whole of it took around five minutes. I had excellent thighs.

One night, the *auteur* brought the lights down in accord with my movement, leaving only a tight spotlight around the face of the pianist, stage right, so that by the time I was on the ground, the area around me was completely dark. My blocking was to roll offstage, which sounds easier than it is. The body is encumbered by arms, which, even when accounted for, make the journey of a bodily roll bumpy enough to throw one off course, particularly if one can't see where she's going. I rolled in the darkness, hoping I was navigating correctly, that my muscle memory would retain the route. After several rotations, my head *thwacked* into the back leg of the piano. Echoing. Resounding. I reoriented myself with this new information and rolled offstage.

During the process, the *auteur* had countless tantrums. "I'm not your father, little girls," he yelled at us once, to which Tracy and I responded (later, in private), "Thank god." He'd pound his fists like a little boy, striking the light board. "Je suis malade!" he'd cry. "Je suis malade!" In the end, we hated him. His jaundiced grief. He was not, by then, sympathetic. But I remember each night twirling, twirling, secretly amazed that my body had been taught to defy gravity.

*   *   *

A spring day in Los Angeles. We'd returned from a trip with our children the day before, a tour of Civil War sites—Gettysburg, Antietam, and others, less famous. I'd barely passed my history classes in high school, where facts and dates were expected to take precedence over narrative. History was memorization: here is the name of the man who lived from this date to that one. He invented, or triggered, or decided. Etc. Etc. Tidy and dry in textbooks. But walking the grounds in Pennsylvania with my sons, aged thirteen and fifteen—on the verge of being the same ages as the men and boys whose blood turned those fields red—it became real to me for the first time. The loss of limbs. The loss of life.

Two years earlier, I'd survived cancer, though *survive* always struck me as the wrong word. I knew people who'd survived. The chemo. The radiation. That was survival. I also knew people who hadn't survived. I knew people who, in years to come, wouldn't survive. But I'd gone to sleep one afternoon, with the assistance of strong anesthesia, and woken up cancer-free. Technically survival, though my role had been entirely passive.

This lovely spring day in Los Angeles, nearly two years after my surgery, I don't recall what we were talking about—me, Jack, the boys—only that we were close and happy. And then, for some reason that I still can't articulate, I pressed a finger into the shin of my right leg, and what appeared was an indentation. Had my skin always reacted this way and I'd only just recognized it?

I pressed my thumb into my left leg to test it: nothing.

Again, on my right: there it was.

It seemed inconsequential, if odd. I Googled the symptom. Then the associated condition. *Lymphedema.* The images that came up were horrific. Elephantine limbs, angry flesh, skin folds, cellulite, disfigurement. A horror movie. My only thought: Get it off me!

Then disbelief.

Then anger.

Then sobbing, sobbing, at the kitchen counter.

*   *   *

The dog's coughing gets worse, yet every morning he's up, his tail wagging. He eats his meal, chews his bone. How much time is left? In my mind, I say goodbye to him several times a day. But he's still here. Still waking. Still toddling into the kitchen for breakfast.

The vet checks his ears. Despite the arthritis in his hind legs, the growth scabbing on his hip, the cough (both cardiac and tracheal), the occasional disorientation, his inability to hear, to see, the ongoing management of his seizures, she tells me he "looks great."

*   *   *

Eight years ago, at a routine appointment, my doctor asked if I'd known my uterus was enlarged. "Probably fibroids," he'd said. At my age, the advice was to let them shrink on their own. I was headed toward menopause within the next few years; the body would take care of things naturally. "Though, be sure to tell me if you're in pain," Dr. S had said.

On my way home, I was reminded of the sharp jolt in my hip, a creak of my body that I'd been living with, hoping it would go away on its own. I wrote Dr. S an email the next morning: *Could this be related?*

It wasn't an emergency, he told me, but he scheduled an ultrasound. The tech spread jelly over my abdomen, moved her wand along my skin, inside my enlarged uterus, not speaking, just the *shhh, shhh* of the machine, retracing her motions over and over until I finally asked—as if a kind of joke—"How many fibroids *are* there?" After a long moment she said, "You don't have any fibroids." Not an ounce of humor in her delivery.

It's not lost on me, now, the waving of the wand, as if she cast a spell that turned me into stone. Or a toad. Or banished me deep under water until something magical could release me into myself again. (Meaning: forever?)

A month later, in the recovery room, despite assurances that the surgery was only exploratory, that my numbers weren't high enough to think it was cancer, the nurse at the head of my bed shouted to someone across the room: "I've got a radical hysterectomy waking up!" (For a while after that, many things were said with exclamation points.) Then she turned toward me. "You've got the most beautiful eyelashes."

The next morning Dr. S visited me with a photo of a white blob, "the size of a tennis ball." I tried to imagine the space it had taken up in my body. How could I not have known? He told me there had been another tumor, smaller, inside this big one. Like a secret. That had been the real danger. That little one. Like some kind of stealth cancer. He recounted how he removed the tumors, the ovaries, my uterus and cervix, fallopian tubes, and—to be cautious—"several lymph nodes." He showed me forty-two staples running up my abdomen, lifting my gown to inspect his work. After he left, a nurse held my hand. "You're going to beat this," she said with tears in her eyes. I was still trying to work out how I'd carried a tennis ball inside my body without knowing.

Radical hysterectomy is a medical term. It's differentiated from a simple hysterectomy or a subtotal hysterectomy or a supracervical hysterectomy by the removal of—in addition to the uterus and ovaries—the upper portion of the vagina, fallopian tubes, and "surrounding supportive structures." It also implies the dissection of lymph nodes. It can take up to two months to recover when the surgery is performed abdominally, and the woman should not lift anything heavy, like grocery bags, for example. Or dogs.

There are no instructions for dealing with the psychological loss of this anatomy. Many people told me I was lucky I'd already had children. That I no longer had any need for my reproductive organs.

Whenever I say it aloud, I can't help thinking, *Wow. Dude. Like, radical.* A silent joke to myself.

*   *   *

We have hundreds of lymph nodes throughout the body. The lymphatics work in tandem with the cardiovascular system, though on somewhat of a different track. (Word is, in medical school, a total of forty minutes is dedicated to the study of the lymphatic system.)

Lymph nodes are the great unsung heroes of the body. They do the work of cleaning out impurities, toxins, sending it all toward the kidneys to perform the final flush. When we're ill, the lymph nodes go into high gear. This is why, sometimes, they'll be enlarged when you have a cold, for example. Or cancer. When cancer gets into the nodes, they become overly effective at spreading it to other parts of the body. During a surgery to remove tumors, the nearest node or cluster of nodes is often removed as well, then tested to see if disease is present. When Jack had prostate cancer, his surgeon took out half of one lymph node; when I had surgery for ovarian cancer, they removed thirty.

It's protocol to dissect lymph nodes, and now that more people are surviving cancer, there's more evidence of lymphedema. It's become, to some extent, an expected outcome. The problem lies in the proximity between nodes. This can make the difference between a working lymphatic system and an ineffective one. The most helpful explanation I've heard is a comparison to a series of stations for an electric train. Each one has only enough power to get the train to the next station in line. Remove some of those stations and suddenly there's not enough juice. The train can go downhill (because: gravity) but it can't get back up. It stops moving, and everything it was carrying (the detritus of your body) gets stuck.

This is what happens in my leg now. All the trains are backed up, swollen with angry passengers. None of them with a sense of humor.

*   *   *

Years after the avocado tree came down, we planted two plum trees. The Santa Rosa can, in the right conditions, self-pollinate, but its chances for bearing fruit are higher with some help from the Satsuma. Both trees bloom each spring with fragrant white flowers, but only the Satsuma has given us plums, juicy and sweet, which we try to harvest before the squirrels get to them. The bees and butterflies do their work, and Jack, too, spends hours with Q-tips, transferring pollen to the Santa Rosa, but no luck. She won't perform on command.

And isn't she enough as she is? Home to finches and bulbuls. An arbor for the dog on a hot day. What more should we expect of her?

*   *   *

An ongoing joke between us: Jack and I speak as if we're the dog, giving voice to what we imagine he might say. It's an intentionally stupid sounding voice, but not without a cynical awareness. *Ha ha*, one of us will say, giving ourselves a slightly stuffed-up quality, like a kid with allergies (which I was). *Ha ha. Still alive.*

*   *   *

For a long time, early in my adult life, I was not kind to my body. I ingested. I inhaled. I mistook sex for love, repeating the error to a dizzying degree. It wasn't unique, my behavior, in the crowd I ran with, though I knew plenty of other people who didn't risk their anatomies, who seemed to have some sense of their right to exist without the aid of a drug or a drink or a body. I did not. I was a splattering of uncontained emotions and desires. The driving force was (I can now name) a need to feel worthy (of what? by whom?)—an amorphous concept, more felt than known. For far too long, I held tight to the idea that to be desired was something other than hormones and availability.

Later, I tried to make up for it, this punishment I'd inflicted on my body (my soul?). I climbed mountains, took up running, tennis, swimming. I eschewed all drugs except for Advil. And when, amidst my transformation, a man showed up whose hunger was tempered with stability, I paid attention. I returned his attention.

What I can't help but wonder now, though, is whether there's a connection. Did I cause my current bodily woes, or would they have occurred in any case? An inevitability of my genetic map.

*   *   *

My father loves to tell the story of my pneumonia when I was two years old, how I had to be placed in an oxygen tent. I don't remember, but he recounts that I said the mist reminded me of his cigarette smoke (Dorals, two packs a day). I was scared to go inside, but he comforted me until I allowed someone to lift me in.

My older son developed pneumonia at age seven. I remember the horror of his screams as nurses tried to place the IV in his tiny veins, the agony (this is the appropriate word) of the decision—after three weeks of worsening symptoms—to have surgery to drain his lung, the near-fainting (both Jack and me) in the hallway after they wheeled him to the OR.

I'd brought his pillow from home in its Superman pillowcase. His small head, hair so blond it looked white, rested against the blues and reds of Superman's cape, which unfurled beneath my son's pale face. I remember this, too: the shadow that he was upon release, having lost a tenth of his body weight.

There's no hidden message in anything, no fairy tale ending. There is just disease. And when we're lucky, a cure.

*   *   *

Jack and I found each other across the country. I moved to New York for him, then he moved to Los Angeles for me. Every time the odds seem against us, we outlast them, mostly because Jack is so steady. I flail against every dimming possibility, worrying, questioning, looking backward, as if the past will reveal anything about the future.

The other night, he made a soup from roasted broccoli. He served it with a squiggle of olive oil, a sprinkling of Parmesan cheese, a touch of salt and pepper ground over the top. What does it mean to be lucky in love? If you'd asked me before I met Jack, I'd have given you the wrong answer.

*   *   *

In the dark, the dog wanders all over the yard in confusion. Even when I guide him back to the stairs that lead to the deck, he backs away, disoriented. And yet, once I've finally coaxed him inside, he goes straight to the dishwasher to lick the dirty silverware. "That's a dog who's very much alive," my friend says.

The coughing is painful. At least, it sounds painful, as if the dog is wheezing out his internal organs. We dutifully give him his medications, the hydrocodone, sildenafil—generic for Viagra. Originally prescribed for the heart, it was discovered to have properties that were otherwise beneficial to men with sexual dysfunction. The dog doesn't seem to be aroused in this way, but I sometimes wonder if that's what's keeping him alive. Not just encouraging the beating of his heart, but a zest, a rush. The thrill of possibility?

*   *   *

I miss shoes. Open toes, mules, ankle straps, heels. Boots stretching to my knees. Shoes that highlighted my pedicure. This is vain and ridiculous, though while I'm at it, I also miss jeans that were meant to be tight yet hung loosely. Skirts that showed off my calves. I thought I could count on my legs, long and shapely as they once were, to carry me through to old age.

Being in public is to be reminded of ankles. I hadn't appreciated how delicate they were until I lost mine. (Just the one.) Swollen in perpetuity. From behind, I look like a model for one of Picasso's bathers. Not the beauties from 1918 with their long torsos and luscious hair, but a decade later, his series of bodies with triangular arms and legs nearly unrecognizable as limbs. No hint of the curves and concavities that delineate the leg's connection to the foot.

I stare at all the ankles. Women in their leggings, or loafers and capris. Ankles are everywhere. Even baggy pants have hems that leave just enough room for a hint of skin. A whisper of bone. I understand why the Victorians swooned. It's a sublime piece of the body. Complex. Elegant. Tapering.

*   *   *

Have I mentioned the hip dysplasia? On the left. Congenital, apparently. The pain set in ten years ago. (If I were a fictional character, it would be too much. And yet, to omit it here would be the lie.) Without the pain from that deformity—undiagnosed until only recently—Dr. S wouldn't have ordered the ultrasound, the tech wouldn't have waved her wand, and deep within my body, unnoticed, the stealth cancer would have grown and grown. So, I'm grateful for the knobby ball of my hip, the not-fully-formed socket.

A trifecta of maladies. Each of their own origin but exacerbating the others. The left hip tries to compensate for the heavy right leg. The weight of the leg compresses the curve on the right side of my spine. My hip and spine compete for the pelvis, twisting it under and back, pulling, causing the many muscles connected to it to tighten into spasms. My walk is Frankensteinish. I try to remember to shift my weight forward, lift the right leg instead of dragging it, release the tailbone so that my hips can swing (if not exactly side to side, then as close as I can get), engage my core muscles, breathe.

Breathe.

A body rolling in the dark.

*   *   *

A chronic condition comes to define you. Even if you resist it, that only makes it more so. A daily reminder of loss. You become acutely aware of what you can't do. Sometimes you do it anyway and cause further pain, further injury. You wear the wrong shoes. You walk for too long (or at all). You stand at a party, sit in the theater, sleep on the wrong side. Maybe you have a good day, you feel almost normal, so you do more than you should and pain engulfs you. Do everything right and it will engulf you all the same. It shapes you despite your best efforts: your gait, your posture, the way you dress. You change what you do, who you see, how you live. You leave the house less often. You're no longer comfortable in your skin, your skeleton. (Maybe you never really were?) Sanity occasionally becomes questionable. You inhabit a body that is yours and not yours, and so, who are you? Or rather, where have you gone?

When you're inside pain, that's all there is. The aperture shrinks. There's no other possibility, no hope, save for (in my case) an atheist's prayer that it dissipates. Your entire being, your place in the world, is only to be in pain.

From the outside, it's both boring and invisible.

Technically, I can do almost anything. I can sit. I can stand. I can walk. It's the pain that limits it. And the inevitable swelling. I sometimes wonder whether it's too much to bear for anyone in my situation or if I buckle easily. I look to others with disabilities for guidance, but most of us are in hiding.

*   *   *

There are a few people who see me, who recognize the *me* that's surrounded by my condition. Jen, with her soft strokes of lymphatic massage; Diane, who patiently adjusts my imbalanced walk; Chi, guiding me through bridges and planks, "Up. Lifting," Chi says. "Up. Lifting." These women who comfort, restore, retrain my body with gentle-firm hands. Gentle-firm words. *Lean to your left. Elevate. Elongate.* They hover above me, around me. The way some people see angels.

*   *   *

Several years ago, Jack and I planted a sapling between the two palms on our parking strip and staked it well, or so we thought. A Sumac, it grew crooked. Despite the bracing post, her trunk bent one way, then another. After a time, she found a kind of equilibrium. Her trunk curved, but she reached toward the sun. Her leaves now provide shelter for robins, sparrows, mourning doves. Squirrels jump from limb to limb.

The palms on either side tower above her, a haven for rats, and too tall to give any kind of shade. I wonder how our tree would regard them. With envy? With sorrow? Her arms reach out to touch them, as if in reassurance. They stand straight, but she's the one to offer her canopy, leafing up and out.

Encouragement comes wherever it's found.

*   *   *

I take the dog out for his evening walk. He goes up the length of two houses and back down again, just enough to smell the outside world, to feel like he's a part of things. Dusk is settling. A clear night. Through the window, as we near the house, I can see lights on in the kitchen. Jack is chopping vegetables for salad, putting a flame under a pot of water, stirring onions, caramelizing them—one of his specialties. The crisp air is tinged with a savory, smoky scent.

Release your tailbone, I think, adding an inch of height when I do. *Shift forward.*

Mercury is visible to my right, Jupiter on my left. *Breathe*, I remind myself. The dog pays no attention to me. He stops to sniff as something catches his interest, then trots ahead when he remembers that it's dinner time. There must be enough light—just enough—for him to be able to make out the familiar shape of our house, the steps, where he waits impatiently for me to open the door, to catch up to him. *Come on, Lady,* he says in my made-up voice. *Life is short.*

EMILIE PASCALE BECK *won the Levis Prize for Fiction in 2022 for her novel,* The Torch Bearer. *Her writing has been published in* Colorado Review, Los Angeles Review of Books, Waxwing, Howlround, *and* LA Stage. *In addition to writing prose, she's a theatre director, dramaturg, and playwright. Her play,* Sovereign Body, *was a finalist for the 2011 Smith Prize. For many years she served as the Literary Manager/Director of New Play Development at Boston Court Theatre, where she directed and dramaturged award-winning world premieres. She received her MFA in Fiction from Warren Wilson.*

(Other Mother.)

River Lucero

Can I sleep? Rain outside. A smaller heap is already sleeping. Small Child next to me. Me heap and Small heap in the bed in the dark room with the rain outside. The world is dimly contoured. Hideous afternoon light sneaking in. Nap time. I can sleep, but not on time. I can't stop thinking when I have time to think. I think one day, I will close my eyes and never know that I existed. No, I don't think so. I know.

*   *   *

A skimming dream. I call them skimming dreams, because you're not really asleep. You're just skimming the surface. You get the imagery and the sensations and the significance, but somehow, you're still awake. Aware.

A maiden is braving the edge of a cliff. Ground is sucking, slop, muddy. Maiden because she's in vestal white. Rain soaked. Maiden because the bouquet of wilted wildflowers she is clutching is bloom-bright. Sharp angles of starved bone. Smiling, deranged. I feel tenderness for how feral she feels. How icy.

*   *   *

Little Child wails. Small Child sleeps. I'm awake. No more skimming. Always when I'm near, I'm yanked back. The wailing pierces my body in places I never knew existed, in places that have yet to exist. Fear or rage or sadness, but more like crawling or burning or pinching. Sometimes, I'm prey. Little Child is predator.

Awake. Big eyes in a dark room. Small Child still asleep. Cherubic in faint, sneaky light. Soft and round and silent. Small Child behaves better than Little Child. Why can't Little Child behave?

*   *   *

Please understand: I am not Other Mother. Like all mothers, Other Mother only lives in me. Waiting. Anybody can live through Other Mother in their mind, but be careful. Some mothers become Other Mother.

It isn't Small Child's fault that Little Child summons Other Mother from where she's hidden, waiting inside of me. When I'm watching Other Mother, I know she's not me. I can't think like me, see like me. I'm somewhere else. I watch Other Mother do things in my mind. She lives my life. I live hers. Other Mother is the rage and the sadness from that rage, is the crawling and burning that doesn't know where else to go, what to do. Sometimes she hurts. Sometimes I think she'll do something too terrible to watch. Still, I watch.

The wailing continues. Another room. Nearby. Other Mother can only take it for so long, before the burning and the crawling makes her burst alive. She only wanted to sleep. She only wanted a life. She wasn't able to sleep. She isn't able to have a life.

Other Mother sits up. I watch. She looks at Small Child. Little Child cries. Sky high crying like crashing cymbals, incessant. Wants attention. Non-emergent. We know all the different cries. Other Mother admires Small Child, envious they can sleep. Affection splits the corners of her eyes. Slowly, the hint of a loving smile. But love can't withstand the burning, the crawling.

Like a pit viper, swift and mean, emotionless. Other Mother strikes with a cheap, bulky pillow that has cartoonish flowers. She holds it over Small Child's face. Shoves down. Muffled noises.

Muted panic. Small Child struggling. Other Mother smiling or crying or both. Other Mother looking placid and crazed. The pillow is taken away. Small Child is blinking blinking, nonplussed. A fancy word for frozen.

(Some people's Other Mothers are murderers.)

The dim room. Shockingly quiet. Small Child looking looking blinking blinking.

Why? Like a marquee fanning across their pupils. Why?

As if Little Child knows, no more wailing. Then, wailing again.

Other Mother rises from the bed. Other Mother feels nothing. Other Mother has a plan. She leaves the room. She walks through the little, pathetic excuse for a hall, littered with the landmines of little feet-killing toys and clean or filthy or somewhere in-between pieces of little clothing. Wailing is louder now, forced and thin. She walks into the wailing room. Little Child has no more wails left, seeing Other Mother. Little Child loves to do this. Scream and summon Other Mother. They have no idea that Other Mother exists inside of mother. That they summon Other Mother with their screams.

Little Child stares. Smiles. Other Mother stares, serene. Smiles back. She knows this act. Shuts the door behind her.

(I can only see the door now.)

(Other Mother whispers, *Why live*? But then again, isn't that all she wants to do?)

*   *   *

Rain outside. Inside, my sleeping heap is awake. Next to me, smaller heap is still sleeping. Small Child. Me heap and Small heap. Dim contours in hideous afternoon light. Nap time. Wailing from the other room, from Little Child. Then silence. Did Little Child feel me summon Other Mother in my skull? No. Other Mother is a secret. Every mother's secret.

*   *   *

Skimming dream. A maiden. Rain. A steep cliff. A bouquet of wildflowers. White clothes. Soaked and clinging. Smiling, deranged.

Happily, maiden walks to the edge. Happily, maiden leaps from the cliff. Happily.

The piercing sound of a child's wailing.

* * *

Awake. Crowded bed. Big eyes in a dark room. Maybe not so big. Never sleeping. No true rest. The eyes get smaller as the world gets bigger and farther away as my life gets smaller as everything gets farther away. Small eyes in a dark room. Once so big in a big world.

I look over. Small child asleep in the faintness. Cherubic. A parted mouth. Tiny milk teeth. Baby fat face. Wailing continues elsewhere. Little Child. Sky high and insistent, clashing and crashing and smashing into me. Attention-seeking, non-emergent. Little Child could wail for hours. Little Child could test its best screams. Little Child doesn't understand things like my hyperacusis. Wailing burning like a blade in my skull.

I admire Small Child. Sleeping Child. Small Heap. Still asleep. Affection that I feel guilty for. I don't feel affection as deeply for Little Child. Some chemicals released from having Small Child placed on my chest. Little Child was not placed on my chest. Little Child was too little. Little Child had to go to the NICU. No costly skin-to-skin. Instead, to a cellblock with cozy cages for babies. Visiting mothers are always weeping, holding their knickknack-sized babies. Never knowing that someday, Other Mother will slither into their skulls, too.

I shift. Kiss Small Child on the cheek, soft and quiet. Lie back. Stare at the ceiling. Where are my chemicals for Little Child? Can't I find them? Little Child makes my skin hurt. I want to love them. I do love them. But the love is different. Little Child never lets me sleep. Hurts my skull. A movie I watched long ago said that love is all a matter of timing. The timing is off with Little Child. Crying when I can finally rest. Awake when I can finally sleep. And me forced to be awake. Awake. Awake.

Can still hear the faint hum of the crying. And then, nothing. Open my eyes. Did Little Child stop crying? Shut my eyes. Yes. Thank you, Little Child. It's fine to sleep. This is nap time. All of us deserve to sleep. You deserve to sleep. Me too. I deserve to drift. I can sleep now. I deserve that strange place between deep dreams and skimming. Uncanny imagery of bone soaked, starved maidens. Their wildflowers and cliffs.

Mom, Little Child says. Somewhere drifting, I hear it. It isn't real. Is it?

Mom. Mom, Little Child says from the doorway.

Too loud, knifing into the room with the word mom. The word *mom* is like an incantation that cuts me each time it's said.

Mom, Little Child says, The sun is *nuclere fooshin.*

I understand the jumbled pronunciation. Half awake. Eyes brimming with tears. It's okay not to rest. It's okay to leave the rain and the white. Open eyes.

Nuclear fusion, I correct politely. Proper pronunciation.

Little Child doesn't attempt to repeat the correction. Only mouths them, practicing.

Do you have to wake up crying? I ask Little Child. Is that your entrance music? Like the *Halloween*, Michael Myers theme? Why not just get up, come in here, or play in your room? Quietly?

Small Child stirs, WHY DO YOU ALWAYS CRY, Small Child rages, GO AWAY.

Little Child whines in high pitch, gratingly, YOU GO AWAY. Awake now. Awake.

*   *   *

The kitchen. Various sources of noise. Clatter. Clink. Boing. Laughter. Small Child and Little Child are playing, endlessly chattering, arguing. Overstimulating cutesy voices of cartoons. Clang. Boing. Clink. What's it like to have a village? To not do this alone? To not feel so isolated, even though I'm surrounded by people when I leave the house? That's the funny thing about isolation. You can be surrounded, swarmed, smothered by people when you go in public, but you're still alone. You can't talk. You lost your voice. Not used to talking.

(To not be stuck? To have time? To sleep? To be rich? To have a fridge full of food?)

I open the fridge. Near empty. A few pathetic jars of unappetizing shit that nobody wants to eat. Doesn't affect me as much anymore, bright sight of a near empty fridge. Common occurrence. First of the month, I'm the best mother that's ever lived. A saint. The fridge is full. Other Mother barely makes an appearance in those first few weeks.

I close the fridge. Open it again. Full of food. A fantasy. That expensive, organic shit from Whole Foods. Ladies with cartloads who never calculate how much things cost fill their carts with this type of shit. But the pizza is cheap and greasy beneath the heat lamps at Whole Foods. Two fat slices for seven bucks.

I shut the door. Open it again. All gone. Nothing to cook. Something easy. Eggos it is.

*   *   *

Spartan living room. Cramped.

Children at the kiddie table by the TV. Eating Eggos and banana slices on gaudy paper plates, drinking water from little kiddie cups that have grins and eyes. Noise is rising, burning again. Getting to me. So many things to do. Places I could've been, seen. Is my heart beating too fast, too hard? Why can I hear it in my ear? When I move, sometimes my chest hurts. Should I have never been born? What's it like to die? I don't want to. I want to outlive emptiness. But sometimes, I don't.

I'm wincing endlessly. Call it the triangle of tension. Neck, shoulders. Can never loosen the muscles. Not since I woke up in the world. Children fight over whose plate is whose. They get up out of their seats. Run. I remind them to eat. Sooner we eat, sooner we can go to the store.

Can we get a cake pop? Little Child asks.

No, I say. We don't have the money.

I wanna cake pop too, Small Child says.

Can I get a cake pop? Little Child asks again. Dad gets cake pops.

He gets money from his parents. We don't get free money, I say.

The vampiric, laughable cost of lawyers. Wonder if it was ever a good idea to reach an agreement about custody in order to avoid the ridiculous, unreachable fees of court orders. No co-parenting with a low-IQ-wrapped-in-red-pill incel. Never liked men, but life and circumstance and fear force us all to blend in, act normal. Low self-esteem. Childhood trauma is a hell of a thing. Embedded like shrapnel. Spend your whole life trying to find the pieces, pluck them out.

I don't even care about cake pops, Little Child says.

Good. You're not getting one anyway. Now eat, I say.

Children sit again, but they don't eat. Entranced by the TV that on occasion makes them quiet. Make them eat. It isn't working. They're loud. They don't eat.

*   *   *

Kitchen. Noise bouncing around in the living room. Small space. Noise bouncing everywhere, no matter where you are.

Few dishes in the sink. Milk cups. More things to do.

Pile of books. Some half-read, dog-eared, stacked on a pathetically painted over, glued, stained, ancient dining table. If only I had time to read. Each book a world a door a window I'm too tired to enter.

Window is above the sink. I gaze out. Beyond the backyard, a field. The rusty bones of a neglected playground. A small, gravel trail to jog on. I reach into the cupboard. Grab some earplugs. Stuff them in. Slowly, they expand. Slowly, the world is drowning. Slowly, the world is happier. Quieter.

I stare out at the field. Watch the jogger. A woman.

*   *   *

But then Other Mother backs up from the window. Back. Back. Back. Peeks at the kids. Other Mother can't hear them, but they're talking. Muted rumble of what they're saying, what they're screaming. Other Mother has an idea. Escape. See, Other Mother isn't always ugly. Isn't always violent. Some people's Other Mothers are worse. Remember that one lady who became her Other Mother, killed her kids. She'd said, *Something exploded in my mind.*

Other Mother slips on her shoes. She is mindful. Makes sure the kids don't see her.

Sneaks out the backdoor seamlessly as somebody sinking into water.

Outside. Fresh and cold and quiet. Soothing. Grass so verdant. Wildflowers. Almost supernaturally bright. Everything is perfect and calling and significant. Everything is free. Other Mother is free now, too. She yanks out the earplugs, tosses them. She walks down, then around the street. She's by the blue skeletal rusty ugly neglected playground. By the field. On the gravel track. Smiling.

Someone is jogging. A woman. Other Mother begins to jog, but then she begins to run. Other Mother thinks of the great alone times of her life. The gorgeous emptiness of before. Before and before and before. Waking up to silence. Watching shows about true detectives and time being a flat circle. No dishes in the sink. Running. Running. Run. No fear of explosions in her mind or becoming Other Mother forever or fear in general, because to have children is to fear for the first time.

She stops by a set of benches. Out of breath. A pack of cigarettes on the bench. Red lighter on top of the pack. Should she? Could be laced. A setup. Pissed on. Been so long since Other Mother has smoked. Other Mother doesn't give a fuck. Other Mother is out of breath, breathing hard, her throat closing, burning. She wants it to burn more.

Lights a cigarette. Sits on the benches table. Coughs. Kinda dizzy already. Smoke worming through blood vessels, beneath the skin. Burning, but pleasant. She yanks as much smoke as she can into her lungs. Deep deeper deepest. She doesn't cough. The sight of the smoke is nice. She's an assassin or a spinster or a changeling or a completely brand new dream. The world goes dim. Other Mother sees the little window she was once gazing out of. Sees someone staring back from it. A sad aberration.

A funhouse reflection.

*   *   *

Kitchen. Noise bouncing around. Small space. Noise bounces everywhere, no matter where you are.

I reach into the cupboard. Grab some earplugs. Stuff them in. Slowly, they expand. Slowly, the world is drowning. A sip of peace.

I watch the jogger. A woman. Someone else out there, too. Smoking on the bench.

Begrudgingly wash the dishes. Hands so dry. Skin tight. Nothing helps. Zombie hands. Hands like the dead. Hands like the damned. More dishes tossed into the sink. Spoons. Children smile. I smile back. Sometimes, I wonder where my real smile went. Buried beneath all the smiles I had to fake. Had to use like punctuation.

Water's shut off. Unnerving silence. Nothing through the earplugs. Some trickle of knowing. Something amiss. I loosen the earplugs. Fingers still wet. Back up. Back. Back. Back. Peek into the living room.

No kids.

Sound of water. Faucet running. Little feet splashing. Laughing.

Through the small living room, stepping on a small, hard plastic landmine dinosaur. Sound of my own shrieking is confined to the inside of my mouth, my skull. Small opening to the hall, into the pathetic excuse for a hall. Bathroom. Threshold of the bathroom.

A swollen pool of water on an already shoddy floor. Wasted squiggles of liquid soap. Wasted snaking lines of shampoo. Imagine a cart full of groceries full of shampoo full of liquid soap. Imagine not having to calculate everything, look at everything for what it is: an expense. What an expensive world.

My iPhone. My old, but expensive to replace, iPhone. In a wet hand. My no-money-to-replace iPhone. My iPhone with text and internet and social media and books and the things that keep my mind away away away when here and here and here is crawling and burning.

My iPhone. Held safely in a wet hand. Ready to plummet into the puddle. Some sacrificial metal and glass and plastic maiden.

*   *   *

In my mind, Other Mother can't control herself. She snaps. Explosion. She grabs the phone. She grabs the nearest child. Is it Small Child or Little Child? It's hard to tell. All children look the same in a snap, in an explosion. All children in the shape of everything that has ever gone wrong or goes wrong or will go wrong. In the shape of all bad. Other Mother goes blind. Forgets. And yet somehow, remembers everything so acutely, that her mind can't focus on anything. Only reflect every painful thing. On and on and on and on.

(Other Mother wasn't always easily summoned. Other Mother had time to germinate, to grow. To find roots and life with every little thing that fed her, you see.)

She grabs, shakes Whichever Child. Shrieks like something keening. Like a feral animal. No words. Just a shriek. Over and over until her throat quits. She pushes the child into the puddle. Crying.

My Other Mother is broken, but not as broken as other Other Mothers. Not always. Today, my Other Mother isn't behaving as badly in the safety of my skull. She grabs both children. Other Mother knows other people have friends and family and help and money and health and ways to feel better. Ways to feel. She flings them into their room. Slams the door. Bangs against the door with her fists. Keening.

You could've ruined my phone. We don't have money! Why? Why!

Always, Other Mother wants to know why, but she never will.

(Mostly, all of life's *Whys* are rhetorical.)

The children are scared. Crying, screaming.

Other Mother runs into the living room. Grabs her car keys. Leaves the house. Door left wide open. Wide open cage. She drives away.

*   *   *

7-Eleven. Other Mother buys cigarettes. Walks out of the store. Door almost hits her. Somebody was holding it open, neglected to look back when they let go. Other Mother is sedate and sound and silent, so calm now. Notices nothing. Running is nice. Free is nice.

In the car, she sits and smokes and smokes and dreams of highways and constellations over Los Cerrillos. She's forgetting something, but she doesn't remember what it is. Maybe she had a home where she loved someone or something or someones or somethings, but when love makes you ill, it's better to forget.

* * *

Threshold of the bathroom. Ridiculous pool of water on the already shitty floor. Wasted liquid soap. Wasted shampoo. My iPhone in a wet hand. Ready to plummet into the puddle. A sacrificial metal and glass and plastic maiden.

Clean it up! I scream.

(It's fine to scream. Don't be so hard on yourself. Sometimes all you've got is a scream. Sometimes the best you can do is scream.)

I snatch the phone before it can be sacrificed.

Go into my own room, which isn't really my own room. Always visited. Slept in. I lie down on the floor, curl up, drying the phone off with my shirt. Phone still works. Can I ever think or breathe or live or dream or sleep, without the guilt of what I see Other Mother doing in my mind? I want what she wants, but I can't do what she does to get it. I test the phone out. Googling, *Mother goes crazy, kills kids.*

Hate that I can almost understand. Almost. I know what can lead mothers to turn into their Other Mother, do things only their Other Mothers would do. One moment you're a screamer. The next you're a murderer. *Something exploded in my mind.* I heard once that the moment you can fully understand why someone would do something terrible, you become that terrible thing, that person. I can almost understand, but I just can't understand. And nobody, nobody talks about it. That's why my Other Mother stays in my skull.

Safe here. Curled on the ground. Fetal curled on the floor. Wishing I could remember the watery red of pulsing safety. The womb. My last moments of happiness.

Hurry, clean it! Small Child says.

No! Little Child says.

Just clean it, okay?

You do it!

Earplugs back in. Sound drains away. Children become only a light murmur.

I'm not the only one who lives through the fantasies of Other Mother. Some become Other Mother. They tangle with Other Mother. Live as Other Mother. Maybe they were always Other Mother. So many Other Mothers.

It's okay to cry. You have to let yourself cry.

Soon, Small Child is peeking in. They walk over, lie down next to me. Cuddle up.

A pile of towels tower on the bathroom floor.

Muffled through the earplugs.

I'm sorry, and then Small Child begins to cry.

Little Child is an immaculate mimic. They repeat Small Child in the same exact tone. They think anything Small Child does is what they're supposed to be doing, I'm sorry.

They're both lying down now. One on each side.

I'm sorry.

Cat noses in. Probably wonders, *What're all these idiots doing?* Leaves. Licks up some water from the bathroom floor.

*　*　*

Later on. Living room. Getting ready.

Get your shoes on, I say.

My room. Sniff the armpits of t-shirts. The crotches of pants. I put on whatever seems clean. No motivation. I like being invisible. Don't like being invisible to myself. Sometimes, I can see myself in the mirror. Smile. Same cheekbones. Strong skeleton. Sometimes, I can't see myself at all. Sometimes, I'm not even there anymore. Where'd I go? I'm right here.

Buy makeup and perfume and nice outfits and only imagine yourself with them on, in them. Living. Imagination will eventually be enough. In those moments, no Other Mother.

Nobody else is ready. No shoes. Whining, fighting instead. Terrible fights lately. Pulling each other's hair. Dragging each other to the ground. Where'd they learn that? I ask them. They answer, *My mind.*

Put on their shoes for them. Someday, I will wake up and I will be alone. There will be no shoes but my own. You'll miss it, they say. But I won't. Not missing something doesn't mean you never cared. Not missing something means you were ready to let it go. Not missing something means that you knew it well enough, while it lasted. The burning. The wanting. Slithering. Emerging.

*   *   *

The mailbox. A community one.

Watch for cars, I say. But the area is rural and bleak and rarely does a car come violently fast enough to endanger anybody not watching.

Small Child and Little Child don't watch for cars. They run laughing across the street. Wonder what it's like to be free. Or what it could've been like. Can't remember being free. Tried to be when I was small, but was reminded with butterfly blade words that there's no being free. Not your own version of it. Just everyone else's. They didn't get to be free. They have to pass it on. I won't pass it on. Hands and fists and hairbrushes and curtain rods and I won't pass it on. Other Mothers.

Place is desolate. Community mailbox rusted, dilapidated. I open ours. Small Child and Little Child are excited.

Did we get money? Small Child asks, but then pushes Little Child out of the way. Little Child begins the high note routine. Whining that pinches my nerves.

The envelope. Two distant relatives, not bound by blood, who care more than most blood ever does. Far, far away from them. Still, they send envelopes. Wouldn't be here if I had a choice. Would be closer. Inside is a card. Disney. Thirty dollars. A note at the bottom: *Buy something nice for yourself. Happy Birthday!*

Birthday. Never had a surprise birthday party. A room full of faces. I know enough people to possibly fit into a room, but they've never been all in one place. *Oh wow!* I'd say. *Thank you so much!* And I'd have no idea what else to say. So I'd cry instead. Seen.

*   *   *

Store. Children making constant noise, asking and asking and asking. Wish I could give give give. Getting essentials. Eggs, milk. Bread. Free food place at the church isn't until Wednesday. First time I went there and they put food boxes into my trunk, I cried when I drove away.

Wine aisle. Top shelf. A red blend. Something nice. *Happy Birthday.* Maybe rosé. Used to be such a big problem. Made everything better. Sometimes, problems make things better, but only for a little while.

*   *   *

Later on. At home. Other Mother has drunk the entire bottle of wine. She is sobbing and laughing and kissing the children. See? Other Mother is for everything. Every wish. Not just ugly wishes. The children are eating dinner at the kiddie table, including Other Mother. Other Mother sits on the floor.

See. Other Mother isn't always feral.

I wish I had more to give. I give you everything I can. I'm a horrible mother. I'm alone. I've always done every fucking thing alone. No help. We're lucky. I was supposed to be someone else. It's too late to be myself by the time I can be myself again. I can't. Find a new mother. A nicer mother. A mother with money and family and friends. A mother with more to give.

Children aren't listening. Too busy being loud chaotic young. Going pee in their plastic potty. Leaving it there for her to clean.

You'll be fine. You'll live, Other Mother says. She stands up. She looks down at Small Child. Small Child is easier. Quieter. Her favorite. Everyone has a favorite. Even when they're not Other Mother. It's harder to say goodbye to Small Child, and so she doesn't say goodbye to either child. Goodbye is in the way she cries and wishes and wishes.

Where you going? Small Child asks.

Front door is already shut. Other Mother has already left. Same thing. Other Mother at 7-Eleven. Buying cigarettes. Sitting in her car smoking. It can't be that hard to run, remake your life. Mothers have been running away ever since they learned how to run. They just don't talk about it.

There's Other Mother far away. On a highway. Always dreaming of highways and darkness and gas stations and shitty coffee and aloneness. A sky smeared with shivering stars. The middle of the desert on a highway. The middle of nowhere, where there's room to think. So much room. Emptiness. Nothing but room.

*   *   *

Store. Children and their constant noise, misbehaving, asking and asking and asking. Other children are so quiet. Mine are loud and free and laughing.

Getting essentials. Eggs, milk. Bread. Free food place at the church isn't until Wednesday. Might not go anymore. Lots of rot. Last time, new slippery looking snake oil man asked if I'd spoken with him before. A bible in his hands. I said, No. He asked if I wanted a bible. I said, No thanks.

Wine aisle. Top shelf. A red blend. Maybe a rosé. It used to be a big problem, but it made everything better. If only things could be better like that again. One day, I'll wake up and I won't be me. I'll be whoever I was before I became.

I get them a cake pop. *Happy Birthday.*

Woman eyes the coven of girl-children, riled in the cart. Older. Pretty. Looks rich.

Are they twins? Woman asks.

Unfortunately, I say. (My joke that nobody likes.)

It goes by so fast! Woman says. (Heard this before.)

Not fast enough, I say. Did you have twins?

No, Woman says. Such a blessing!

Yes, such a blessing.

(Such a fucking blessing.)

*   *   *

Kitchen later. Making sandwiches. Chewing the crust off. Spitting the crust into the sink.

Can we listen to a song? Little Child asks.

Sure, I say.

The Dream On song, Small Child says.

You got to lose to know how to win, but sometimes, you just lose and lose so much that where you should be winning gets further and further and further away.

I play the song from my phone. Children spin and dance around and I dance too and Small Child and Little Child try to dance like me.

DREAM ON.

D R E A M O N.

DREAMON.

*   *   *

Chaos in the bathroom later. Loudness. I brush the children's teeth. We go into the pathetic excuse for a hall. I take out Small Child's hair band.

Go put it in the silver cup, I tell them.

No! It's dark! Small Child with wide eyes, shaky.

You can do it. It's not that dark, I say.

The silver cup is on the kitchen table. Illuminated by the hall light.

Little Child imitates the shakes, the big eyes. Small Child is doing these things, so Little Child must do these things.

Stop copying, I say to Little Child.

Small Child whines. The sound of it is so much less irritating than when Little Child whines. Small child rarely whines.

I can't, Small Child says. It's too dark. Please!

You're creating a fake boundary, I tell Small Child. A boundary of what you can see, and what you think you can't see, and in the daytime you aren't afraid of this boundary, because you can see everything. You're only scared of what you think is in the dark, because you think you don't know what's there, inside of it. But you do. You saw it all day.

When I'm older, Small Child says.

(I'm not sure what they mean.)

Every decade of your life there will be a lie you tell yourself, I say to Small Child. When you get into the next decade, you finally see what the lie was, but only after the decade where you believed the lie. I used to think the dark had monsters in my first decade, too. And then in my second decade, I knew nothing was there. That in this world, the real monsters are—

Mom, it's too dark, Small Child says.

I wish I could finish thinking. Thinking is the problem. Wanting to think. A long stretch of me thinks, thinking.

The silver cup. I can see it from here. It's on the kitchen table. Next to the window—worlds of books.

If you go, I say, I'll give you the red badge of courage.

Both children perk like meerkats. Alert and alive and curious. The what? Their expressions beg. Mouths agape.

What's the red badge of courage? Small Child asks.

You'll see if you go put the hair tie in the silver cup, I say.

Small Child and Little Child hold hands. They creep through the living room. The kitchen. Cautious and watchful. Small Child runs to the silver cup, throws the hair tie in. They both run back.

I bend to hug them both.

See? Good job, I say.

Now I can have the red badge of courage, Small Child says.

Now I can have the red badge of courage, Little Child says. Near exact mimic.

Stop repeating her, I say. She was more scared than you. She deserves the red badge, but you went with her. You helped. Helping people takes courage.

Where's the red badge? Small Child asks.

The spare room, I say.

They gasp.

We go into the spare room. They aren't allowed in the spare room. Boxes and broken things, castaways. Things to throw away. When there's time. When there's money for junk haul. For now these things live in the spare room. I get a small box from inside the closet. Take out a brand new red lipliner.

What is it? Small Child asks. Makeup?

Cap off, I kneel down. Where's your heart? I ask.

Here, Small Child points.

Shirt is pulled down, just enough. I draw a heart on their upper chest. I draw one on Little Child, too. They're happy. Proud.
But it'll wash off, Small Child says.
Then you'll have to earn it again, I say.
Small Child reaches over to Little Child's heart, smears it.

RIVER LUCERO *was raised in a superstitious household, which might explain the lifelong interest in stories and poetry that flirt with realism and tiptoe into horror. Always juggling a handful of creative projects, the current task is to unleash a novel into the world. And to make sure it has plenty of other work to keep it company.*

The Real Boys of Summer

Jillian Weiss

Summer 2013

An aging truck driver and I wait for rides as the luggage carousel slithers in never-ending rounds. Dallas Fort Worth is the second largest airport in the United States. I wonder if that's why there aren't many people around: there's so much room to spread out. I eat my bag of vending machine Cheetos and think the truck driver looks like Santa Claus. I text my boyfriend to make myself look busy, but Santa talks to me anyway. He's going to drive a truck from Dallas to somewhere up north. He asks what I'm doing in Texas. I've come to be a teaching assistant for an academic summer camp, I say. I've never been here before. He says I look young and tells me about his affairs with his high school history and English teachers.

"And now," he says, "I'm dating a taxi driver the same age as my son."

That's interesting not because of the age gap but because of their professions. Perhaps their relationship will survive because they both understand a life behind the wheel, and I wonder if all the loops back and forth across the country or to and from the airport make them feel they aren't aging at all but twirling in place and time.

My boyfriend texts back that he misses me already. I am glad, but I do not miss him. I like him very much, but I love this adventure.

My shuttle arrives, and I say goodbye. Santa is unsure when his truck will show.

*   *   *

I'd heard there'd be tarantulas in Sherman, Texas, and not much else. Upon my arrival at Austin College, I realize this tarantula tale is more than just myth. Every now and then I see the thick, soft arachnid sitting in the middle of the sidewalk, declaring itself to me like a teenager at a debutant ball entering society: *Here I am.*

Two of the youngest teaching assistants find tarantula holes, fill the holes with water, and watch the tarantulas crawl out to be caught or killed. They do not recognize this as cruelty.

Every building on campus is made of sand-colored bricks, which match the wide cement pathways. On a sunny day, which is nearly every day, the sun reflecting off the ground is blinding. One afternoon, I spot a tarantula in the middle of a bright path and touch it with a stick. It doesn't move. Its legs curve inward like a claw. Perhaps it was trying to dig up the ground as it died.

Tarantulas used to exist for me in scary stories and nightmares only, but now there's one motionless beside my foot: an object from another realm washed up on this reality's shore.

*   *   *

Henry is dancing by himself on the way to the dining hall. Pale arms stick out of a colorful tank. He turns around, sees me, takes his earbuds out, and shouts something. Both of us keep walking toward the dining hall, but he's now walking backward. He shouts something again. I don't understand. He waits for me to catch up, and I push through heat to reach him. He tells me that Kanye West is a genius.

His hair is white in the sun, and his beard is sparkling. He is as bright as this campus and only nineteen years old, four years my junior. This feels like a very large gap. When I was entering college, he was entering high school.

The second time I speak to him, I'm driving his five thirteen-year-old charges to the bowling alley. Henry doesn't have his driver's license yet. In the car, he tells me that his spirit animal is a goldfish. I tell him that my spirit animal is a seal, but I don't tell him that I only know this because of a school assignment. I am already forming an inaccurate version of myself for him. He says, "I can already tell I'm going to miss you when we leave." I think about how weightless he must feel after he says, instantly, what he's thinking. I work my sentences like over-kneaded dough.

Days later, Henry yells my name in the dining hall, and we meet by the soda machines. "Can I hug you? Is that all right?"

We hug. Our students watch. He wears grey pajama-like pants printed with the repeated pattern of a circuit board. When we go out to eat later that week, he orders three different fancy drinks, no food. When we go to Target, he buys a giant, superfluous pillow. In the evenings, he dances around the lobby with his arms in the air. He follows his desires. He is a revelation. He is the free spirit my mother always wanted me to be.

He tells me about his dreams, which he details on his Tumblr. I listen feverishly, dreaming of him dreaming of me. Mid-dream narrative, he notices my protuberant spine, and I lean forward, ask if he wants to feel it. This me—this awkward spine, this asking him to touch—is the real me. I direct his hands to the peaks of highest elevation. "Wow," he says. "I feel it," like he's talking of a change in air pressure.

*   *   *

One afternoon, I take my writing students on a walk. Everywhere, the ground is flat and beige. The pale sidewalks are wide. We approach a crater that's tiered like the seats of an amphitheater. I realize that it will be filled with water and become a fountain. I tell my students to discard their pads of paper, run around the rim, and flap their wings. Be birds! They instantly beat the air with arms like water pumps, their decorated Converse shuffling against concrete, and I feel unreasonably happy. I am amazed that they followed my direction. I am amazed that I get to know them. I am also delighted that I get to live on the precipice of romance again, which I am always teetering into and out of, but often, as in this case, only in my mind. This is not cheating, I tell myself. It is the contentment of existing in unfulfilled dreams, and Texas is wide-open, wondrous, and packed with places to direct my yearnings.

In the second week of camp, I spend the days waiting for Henry to appear. Every day is like the nighttime, and he is the ghost in my house: every creak is blamed on him; every footstep, he is coming to get me. I am more present than I have been all year, living on constant alert. I remember the truck driver and his girlfriend, and I believe now that four years is not an age gap at all. Though he is young, he is already who I aspire to be when I am old.

But I have a boyfriend; he is kind and gentle, and I thought, recently, that I might marry him. He emails me a poem about the distance between us this summer. He is showing me that he can be interested in writing. The problem is not that it is a bad poem but that when I read it, I think more about the poetic craft than his sentiments.

*   *   *

The instructors and TAs go to downtown Sherman, which is a quaint square and two or three blocks of restaurants and businesses. We bring our own booze to an Italian restaurant and for two dollars, the waitress opens the bottles. I notice that no one is walking outside. After eating Italian, we go to the bowling alley for karaoke night, but I do not sing. Remember: I am not an uninhibited person. We pack into cars on the way home and roll down the windows.

I talk to my boyfriend every other evening. We Skype twice, but this makes him feel even further away from my current reality: He is a television show I am watching and can turn off at any time. This summer does not feel part of my other, distant life.

This summer is a portion of time from another universe coughed up from my throat like a delicious lump of food.

*   *   *

Henry and I play Spades with a few coworkers. We are partnered together. How lucky. It turns out that we are good at Spades. On another evening, we have no coworkers to play with and so we each get on our computers and find a pair of people to play online. We stay up until 1:30am, facing each other across a small table, united against phantom competitors. On the final play, we lose.

We hug. We have tears in our eyes.

*   *   *

My students are oblivious. They think I should date the anatomy instructor. His name is Cain but they call him Vampire because he's from eastern Europe. They call me Genie because I wear long skirts. Together, we are Genie and Vampire. We are fiction.

When I tell my students that Cain has a girlfriend and I have a boyfriend, they say, "But this isn't real life. Whatever you do here doesn't count when you get back to the real world."

The scent of this lingers. It is terrible and tempting. "That's not how it works," I tell them. "We have a responsibility to the people who aren't here."

This does not dissuade them. During the last week, there is a dance, and they make Cain and I waltz. Henry is behind the DJ table. We have stayed up late together every night, computers in our laps, shielding our hands from one another. I wonder what he is thinking, and I wonder about my students' theory. Perhaps, precisely here, my actions do not impact the real world. I also wonder if time travels slower across all this land, if the truck driver is still waiting for his ride at DFW, if a tarantula takes years to dry up in the sun.

After the dance, I change clothes in my dorm, and wait on a couch in the lobby. "Hi, Jilly," Henry says, and lays his head in my lap. I think that I do not love him but that I am enchanted by him. We hold hands for forty minutes as staff walk quickly through the room chasing children, making photocopies, or trying to find missing keys. We hear the pitter-patter of feet above our heads, out of sight. I am leaving soon to TA a different summer course at Texas A&M, many hours south. Most staff will be staying here to teach a new set of students, but our employer needs me elsewhere. I will miss Henry's hands and the feeling of waiting for him to arrive.

*   *   *

On our very last night, we sit beside each other in the back seat of a car, having chosen to leave the bowling alley/karaoke night early. The windows are down, of course, and his fingers travel over my hands like a band of pilgrims looking for somewhere to settle down, their heads testing the pillows of my palms.

*   *   *

In the morning, on the drive to my next assignment, I am struck by the empty space in Texas. I no longer see such space as a graveyard but an offering. There is so much land to give, so much air, so many fields and atmospheric spaces presented to us in open truck beds. Should I reciprocate with my own offering? Can this be it?

Compared to Sherman, the number of people and things to do in College Station is initially alarming. There are too many options. I walk the vast campus alone at night, thinking of Henry, thinking of my boyfriend. I see the tree that's famous for cursing you into loneliness if you walk under its branches by yourself but grants love if you walk under with someone else. It's enormous, and both sides tilt down in gentlemanly bows.

Two days after I break up with my boyfriend in North Carolina, I walk barefoot under the tree to prove the theory wrong.

I read my boyfriend a letter over the phone. It was a terrible hour. He tried to scratch himself out of the breakup with words and remembrances, and I felt I was watching a tarantula die right in front of me, and I cried, couldn't do anything about it, and his legs turned into a claw. I tried to believe I was far, far away; it was easy to picture Texas rotating above the earth like an extra moon.

*   *   *

I still talk to Henry online in the early hours of most mornings. We play Spades. I think that our relationship is an early morning and nothing else, a beginning stuck in the first few hours of its cycle. The sunrise, the sunrise, the sunrise.

The weeks pass slowly. Daily, I push a student in a wheelchair six blocks from her dorm to our class. While we sweat in the heat, she talks endlessly of John Green novels. I field messages from my ex. I hear that he knocks on my parents' doorstep and hands them the record player that I gave him for his birthday. I get drunker than I've ever been; I repeatedly ask for Irish Car Bombs at the bar because this seems to garner positive attention.

After the last dance at Texas A&M—at which I slow danced to Lana Del Rey with a dark, slim twenty-one-year-old—the teachers and TAs walk back to our dorm through a muddy field and a fountain. My dress is bright blue, sequined, and floor-length, so I hold the bottom away from the dirt and water, and it sheds glitter on my palms. We walk through an underpass and the lights blare gold, and the university marching band is practicing in the giant stadium beside us, loud brass slicing drama into the summer, and I think that everything is romantic—too romantic.

*   *   *

After changing into casual clothes, we go to Daisy Dukes where BOOTS AND BIKINIS THURSDAYS is never unadvertised. The words are stamped on a white marquee above the entrance. It's a club inside a barn-like exterior, adorned with an enormous disco ball in the rafters you can almost touch from the walkway. We dance a little, but mostly watch.

Out of curiosity, he tells us, the neuroscience teacher went to Daisy Dukes on BOOTS AND BIKINIS THURSDAYS, but there were only old men on barstools inside, their fingers probing their drinks, their hopes not yet lost. The bikinis could still arrive. The bikinis could still arrive.

*   *   *

The bikinis would never arrive—but it was Texas, so the waiting didn't seem so long. The sunrise, the sunrise, the sunrise. The slow agelessness of the summer filled the old men with hope. They could be young again, or perhaps they were never old. The largeness makes the churning slow.

Intermission

Outside of Texas, life accelerates with dizzying speed. I begin grad school on the coast of North Carolina. In the daytime, in lobbies and courtyards and in small, plastic chairs, I meet dozens of people who are all cooler than me. I buy my first car. I move into an apartment that is too close to campus and the three, male undergrads who live above me stash their tiny dog on the porch above mine and droplets of its urine ski down our sliding glass doors.

The earliest class that I have is at 11am, so I can afford to spend many evenings and early mornings on my computer with Henry. I roll into the understanding that Henry is a real, whole person, and that he has real interest in me. I have somehow extracted him from the unreality of summer. One night, he buys a plane ticket. I imagine that it is an impulse buy. I assume he won't get on the plane.

But here he is, at the airport, in a thin grey sweater. He puts his duffel in my trunk. Though it's midnight, he suggests buying milkshakes on our way back to my apartment. I happily follow his desires. After milkshakes, we kiss for the first time and then kiss many more times. His kisses are all different. He hardly repeats the same movements. I find my lips tracking the motion of his lips more than sinking into the pleasure of kissing. His hair is soft and receding.

We sit on the beach, walk the pier as light posts ignite. We eat at Chilis. We throw a frisbee. We do not speak of dating. He lives very far away. We face each other in my tiny twin bed. His eyes are far apart and as delicate as daisy petals.

Summer 2014

This time, I wait for my airport shuttle outside. A polite British man talks to me about his business travels as I vigorously fan myself with my used boarding pass. I'm wearing a solid white dress with spaghetti straps. When I get to the campus in Sherman, two hours later, I match the pavement. Everything is how I remembered—big and blonde, quiet and bright.

Except the enormous new science building has been finished; the fountain filled; I have been promoted from TA to instructor; and this year, instructors will not live in the dorms with the students and residential staff but in apartments across the road from campus.

I do not see a tarantula on my walk to the apartment, but I do feel the familiar flatness and vastness of space: the generous sidewalks, the short and sparsely planted trees that tiptoe into the horizon.

*   *   *

Henry is not returning. It was never his plan. In the spring, we both started dating students at our respective schools. Mine dissolved, but his is lasting. I think I am okay with this, but he is still a reason I have returned here. I need to test the truth of dreamscape Texas.

A friend from last summer is here, and I make plenty of new friends to spend my free time with. The other instructors and I congregate in apartments to help one another invent lesson plans. Most of us have or are acquiring master's degrees in our chosen fields but have little teaching experience. We go to the bar together and to the grocery store to stock our fridge with snacks, and we order pizza while planning collaborations between our classes. As I return from teaching every evening, I stop in the parking lot of the apartment complex and take photos of the sky. Here, it is soft and wide. It is a king-sized bed made with pastel sheets. It is the dream that I remembered.

*   *   *

Then late one evening, long after the colors all bowed to darkness, Henry calls.

I am lounging on a sofa chair in my colleague's apartment, eyeing the purple bruises blooming on my legs from unsuccessfully trying to pull myself into a boat earlier that day. Nine other teachers and I rented a two-story pontoon on our day off and drove it on a giant lake in Oklahoma. We poured beer down the holes of one-dollar pool noodles and into our mouths. I swing danced with a handsome TA on the second level while a bag of white wine sloshed around on the floor. I drove home because I was the only one sober enough to. There was nothing to see but cows, horses, and cornfields as flat as the ocean. We listened to the Red Hot Chili Peppers while the wind dried our hair. I felt Texas's slow breath.

"I have to take this call," I say to my friends in the room, and I run barefoot into the parking lot. Henry has never called me before. We text. We type online while playing Spades. We do not call.

"How's Texas?" Henry asks. His voice is light but filled with purpose like the feet of a dancer.

I tell him it's great but exhausting. I tell him it's different. He says that's good. He says he's not doing well. He calls me Jilly. He is the only person, aside from my younger brother, who calls me Jilly. He says that there was an accident last night. He says that his father was in an accident last night. He says that his father was riding his bike home and was hit by a car. He says his father is dead.

There is the distant rumble of a train. I am sitting under a streetlight as if I am the star of this show.

"Henry," I say.

"I wanted to tell you."

I do not know what to say next. I only feel capable of receiving. I ask him about the rest of his family, which is a stupid question. They are not doing well. I tell him that I want to hug him. This is always true. I ask if he wants to talk. He asks if I want to talk. He says everything is weird. He says we should play Spades online sometime soon. He says that he is sorry to tell me this. I tell him that I am sad to hear it but not sorry he told me. I think that he wants something from the dream version of myself, and I am unable to deliver. He says goodbye. I say goodbye. His voice blows out.

*   *   *

I pull the skin of my face backward toward my ears.

I stand still, and then I jog. I knock on my coworker's door. It's almost midnight. An empty pizza box is on the kitchen table. I return to the sofa chair as if the world were still the same, but nothing is the same. I was crazy to think that time had slowed the summer before. We are always moving. This chair, which I sat on minutes before, is introducing me to a new Earth. Every second the world whispers welcome. Before you can say thank you back, another welcome comes. My blooming bruises are rotting petals now, the grey earlobes of a corpse.

*   *   *

The next day, I research the death of Henry's father, how he was knocked from his bike by a drag racer, how he was killed on impact, how the car didn't stop. A headline calls his father a "safety conscious cyclist." Henry and his father have the same exact name, so Henry suddenly exists all over the internet. He catches Texas— my moon—on a fishing line and reels it back to Earth.

*   *   *

More sadness falls. One of my writing students threatens the lives of other girls and is put on watch, and there is an incident of assault between two coworkers. Searching for lightness, I ride with a van of instructors to Lone Star Lanes, where we sang karaoke and Henry asked about my spirit animal, but the building has been burned down. It looks like a charred game of tic-tac-toe.

Days later, I look up the menu of the Italian restaurant that charges you to open your own alcohol, but it has closed. Thwarted by these defeats, we go to a Mexican spot with incredibly cheap beer and the biggest and fattest quesadilla I've ever had, but it's boarded up and empty. I remember that on our last visit, my coworker had asked the waitress how she was doing, and she answered, "Not too good."

*   *   *

I spend many nights sitting on the curb behind our apartment building with coworkers Kyle and Kushal, the psychology and web programming instructors, while they smoke cigarettes, and we stare into the cornfield across the street. Occasionally, they pass me a lit cigarette and I take a drag. I have never smoked before. It feels like both a form of communication and something to do with silence. Right in front of us, before the field, is an abandoned building, long and narrow like a train car. We talk about checking it out, but we never do.

One night, Kushal sits on the curb beside me to tell me about his female conquests at his old workplace. "One time a girl gave me a look, like this, right in the eyes, and asked if I wanted to do it, so I agreed, and we went into the office. I used to not have this belly, you know."

I have learned that when Kushal is sad about his girlfriend breaking up with him, which she is currently doing in stages over the phone (between bouts of phone sex, he tells me), he exaggerates his love life or dreams about his future women. He reminds me of the truck driver I met at the luggage carousel. While Kushal is in his bedroom arguing with his girlfriend, Kyle and I sit in the living room and watch films with lots of dialogue.

Kyle is dark haired and broad chested. He loves to dribble a basketball by himself and often eats alone in his room to get away from the hundreds of people in the dining hall. He is my closest companion, but the movies remind me of Henry, whose father is dead. Nevertheless, every day I move closer on the couch to Kyle, perhaps just so I might have found something at the end of the long road of lost things.

*   *   *

The Sunday after Henry's call, I watch his father's memorial service. It's live streamed on a tiny, pixelated video screen. The Presbyterian

Church is large and filled; some people appear to be standing. I learn that he was a war veteran, a Harvard graduate, a business entrepreneur, and an ice cream and St. Louis Cardinals fanatic.

Henry walks to the podium near the end of the service. Although he is a small, blurry rectangle with arms, I can hear his voice. He speaks of his relationship with his father through their life playing games together. It is a clever narrative through which to tell their story. He speaks very quickly but clearly, and the images he gives of his father are so precise that when I cry, it is not only for Henry's loss but for the world's loss of Henry's father.

Henry steps down from the podium and his sister steps up. His sister just got into Princeton University and wants to be a pastor. Henry can be anything (he's majoring in psychology, neuroscience, and philosophy, has a job in design, and won a national chess championship as a middle schooler) but had expressed interest in being a librarian. I love this about him, and I love him for not being me, a twenty-four-year-old sitting in Sherman, Texas, poking the smoking logs of our strange affection while also igniting a second fire.

*   *   *

Last summer, Henry got a tattoo at a tiny parlor near the campus. This was after I had left, so he sent me a picture: a lantern on his outer arm. I touched it when we shared a bed in North Carolina.

A week after his father's funeral, I go to the same tattoo parlor. I've had a tattoo in mind for years. As the needle is scarring my skin, I ask my tattoo artist if he tattooed a lantern on a young man's upper arm last summer. He did, he says.

A thought settles: Texas, where time moves so slowly, has finally granted me an ending. Henry and I have been tattooed by the same man. We have been grounded to this earth by the reality of our kindred skin. We are both real, and we were not made for each other.

*   *   *

An evening of my last week, Kyle, Kushal and I lay down on the campus's empty basketball court. Tonight, they feel like my family. The court is cool. The sky is full of stars.

I think about death, but mostly love, because I am always falling for people. Tomorrow night, I think that I will probably kiss Kyle. I think that I would like to kiss him for a long time and then say goodbye.

I think about how I inject fantasy into my perception of the world. This explains slow-motion Texas and the other planet-ness of Texas. This is not because I'm bored of my life's offerings; I am sincerely and regularly amazed by the world. Like the tarantula, everything that I've never seen or experienced before has a magical quality when it first appears: *Here I am!*

A breeze passes, and I am a feather ready to be lifted. And I see the stars, so bright in Texas, so bright they are throbbing—just look at them—like giant wounds in the sky. They are brighter than I've seen anywhere else in the world. But is that true? I'm being too romantic again. I'm not seeing the reality of Sherman, Texas. There should be a consequence for this, just as there should be a consequence for breaking up with my boyfriend through the phone and holding another man's hand. My actions matter. I understand now. You cannot stop time without consequences. Time must balance out. Perhaps I am the reason businesses are dying and people are sad. Time sped up to make up for last summer's stillness! Perhaps Sherman has been forced, by me, to deteriorate at a faster rate!

A wisp of smoke from Kushal's cigarette floats through the black night.

Do you see how my ridiculous mind bends? Always curving back to me. I am, like the truck driver, going in never-ending rounds.

Forgive me, Texas.

As the smoke drifts, the stars come back into focus. Surely, they are the brightest I've ever seen. Surely, they cannot be merely my invention.

JILLIAN WEISS *is a writer and teacher based in North Carolina. Her essays have been published in* The Missouri Review, Fourth Genre, Michigan Quarterly Review, *and elsewhere. She teaches creative writing at RJ Reynolds High School in Winston-Salem where she lives with her librarian husband and three cats. Find her online at www.jillianweiss.com*

My Own True Name

Vicky Grut

The old woman's flat is on the fourth floor of a red-brick block in a good neighborhood, not flashy but I can tell it's expensive. "I don't know why you're here!" she shouts. She is tiny, sitting like a bundle of sticks in the middle of her reclining armchair, but her voice is strong.

"Your son has asked me to come and help you," I say. "He is concerned about you, Rita."

Her son is so concerned that he lives on the other side of the world and pays someone he's never set eyes on to look after her, though to be fair, he thinks I'm the one who cared for his aunt in her last days. That was a friend of mine from church.

When I first came to London, I was a nanny for a rich family, the Fishers. The girl was ten when I started, the boy eight, and the youngest just a baby. I was with those children night and day for four years. I saw them grow. I fed them and wiped their tears and taught them things. They were like my own flesh and blood. But when the youngest started school, the mother said they didn't need me any longer. She told me she was going to work from home and take care of all the things I'd been doing. I knew this was a lie.

139

The real reason was that she could see that the youngest boy had come to love me best and she couldn't bear it. She wanted me gone.

If I had kept my mouth shut she would have helped me to find another family to go to, but I was upset. I spoke my mind. So she threw me out right away. I spent a week sleeping on night buses until someone at my church said I could stay with her until I got back on my feet.

Rita's son thinks my name is Ann. My friend's real name is longer and more beautiful, but these people lose heart if you ask them to remember anything complicated.

"My mother doesn't need much, Ann," he said in our telephone interview, "just a bit of help with the housework, some cooking, someone to talk to. She's very independent."

Four hours a day, six days a week. Who can live on that? Plus, the money has to go through my friend's bank account and she will take some of it for her trouble. I don't have a choice. I've told my parents that I can't send them anything for a while. This is just a start.

*   *   *

Rita watches me as I move around her sitting room with a dust cloth. Someone else must have been doing this work before me. I can see where they dusted and where they let it pile up: behind the ornaments, on window ledges, on top of the television set. It's a big flat. Some of the dust is piled in layers, like cloth.

"How old are you?" she asks. "Forty? Fifty? Sixty? I can't tell these days."

I smile and shake my head. "Old enough," I say.

"Where do you come from? Colombia? Venezuela? Brazil? Are you illegal?"

Illegal? Wasn't I born on God's earth, just like her? But we can't have that conversation. I know that. So I say nothing.

"Are you married? Do you have children?"

I pretend not to hear.

I did have a child once, when I was very young. I had to leave him with my mother while I went to the city to work. He got ill and God took him before I could get back home. That was a long time ago. I have looked after many others since, and for the past four years I had those beautiful, borrowed children, but now their mother has taken them back. I know the littlest one will be longing for me as I long for him. He'll be crying, especially at night. If I close my eyes, I can still feel the softness of his hair, the pressure of his little fingers on my arm. I think of the way his head breaks out in a fine coating of sweat as he drops off to sleep. Who will wipe his forehead now so that he doesn't catch cold? These feelings are painful. But I know they will fade in the end.

I don't share any of this with the old woman because it's none of her business. I smile at her in a false way. "What would you like for lunch, Rita?"

"Call me Mrs. Barker," she says, snapping her dentures. "Not hungry."

If Rita doesn't eat, God will take her, and I will not get paid so I must do my best.

"I will ask you again later, Rita," I say. "Now I hoover."

"Mrs. Barker," she says. "And don't bother. I do my own housework." Even she doesn't really believe that.

*   *   *

After five days in the job, my phone rings. It's a Friday evening. I'm on a city bus full of people as tired as dogs, standing between a man with a lot of parcels and a woman with a baby in a pram. It's a struggle to get the phone out of my pocket. I'm hoping it will be one of my friends calling to invite me somewhere, but the screen says: Craig. This is the name of Rita's son.

He wants to know how I think it's going. "What's your impression?"

I don't say that his mother doesn't seem to like me any better yet. Every day she tells me she enjoys her privacy. And she always complains about my food. It's too salty, too bland, too tough, too wet, too dry. I can never get it right.

"Your mother is a strong person," I say. "She has many opinions. But her body is weaker than she likes to think."

"She's almost ninety," he tells me, and he leaves a gap for me to say: *Wow!* or *What an incredible age!* But I don't feel saying any of those things, so I just wait.

I imagine him in a clean office, leaning back in an expensive chair while he takes these few minutes to ease his conscience. Surely he can hear the catastrophe of noise around me? The shrieks of the teenagers running upstairs, the hiss of the doors, the roar of the engine as the bus takes off again. But even if he hears he probably doesn't understand. This is the sound of *my* time, and he is stealing it from me.

"It's early days, isn't it?" he says. "I guess we can't expect too much, can we?"

I don't know why, but this makes me even more angry. Can't *expect* too much? I used to be top of my class at school. I was the best at spelling, the best at reading and mathematics. I could have gone to university if the situation had been different. Expect! And *we*? Who is this *we*?

Next to me, the baby in the pushchair wakes up and begins to scream. I glance down at its purple, sweating face.

At the other end of the phone, Rita's son is still talking. "Do you mind, um—?" I can hear he has forgotten that my name is supposed to be Ann. "Do you mind if I check in with you like this, every now and then? Occasionally? For an update?"

"If you want," I say. Anything to be rid of him.

*   *   *

When I arrive at the start of the second week, I notice a bad smell. At first I think it's because I forgot to empty the kitchen bin on Saturday. But the closer I get to Rita, the more I can smell it. I see that the dress she's wearing looks a lot like the one she had on last week. Maybe not just a lot like, maybe exactly the same. How did I not see this before? Why didn't her son let me know? This woman can't wash and dress herself anymore.

"It gets so hot in here," I say. "How about I help you take a shower and we change your clothes?"

Silence.

"You will feel more comfortable."

She'd like to tell me to go to hell, but her longing to be clean is stronger. Without a word, she gets up from her chair, grabs hold of her walker and leads the way to her bedroom where there's a bathroom with a walk-in shower I didn't even know about. All this time I've been cleaning the other bathroom and the toilet off the hallway. It's a very big place.

We pick a fresh set of clothes from the cupboards and move to this bathroom.

At first, I feel a strong resistance. I don't want to touch this person. She doesn't like me. I'm not sure I like her. But once we begin, all the steps lay themselves out in my mind and the task doesn't seem so difficult anymore. How many little bodies have I not bathed over the years? Why should this be any different.

I adjust the shower temperature so that it's not too hot and let the water run while I get her undressed. I help her onto the shower stool and she sits quietly while I soap and sponge her flanks, her neck and breasts and belly, her arms, her long crooked back. I kneel down to soap her feet and between her toes. Then I wash her fine grey hair and rinse, rinse, till every part of her is shining.

"All done, Mrs. Barker," I say. Today she has earned her title.

I turn off the shower and cover her in towels. I dry her bit by bit, then dress her in the clean clothes, and when it's done, we are both very tired. I help her over to the bed and she's asleep in a second. I'm going to have to wake her before I leave to make sure she eats. Next time, I say to myself, I should do things the other way around: food first, then washing. We are learning how to do things, Rita and I.

*   *   *

Some days later, when I let myself in, I hear voices coming from the sitting room. As usual, Rita is in her reclining chair. Nearby, on the sofa, is a large woman in a navy pantsuit. She doesn't get up. She gives me a long, careful look, the kind of look a butcher might give a sheep.

"You must be Ann."

"Yes."

Is she a social worker? A nurse? My friend has warned me to be very careful with such people. They will be suspicious. They might ask me for qualifications, certificates, police checks.

"Perhaps you could make us a cup of tea, Ann," says the woman. "How do you take it these days, Mother? Still three sugars? No wonder you don't have any teeth left."

Rita jerks her head at me. "She knows."

"I'll have mine black, please, Ann, not too strong, no sugar, and with a slice of lemon if there is such a thing."

I tell her that Mrs. Barker's son does her shopping online. He does not order lemons.

The woman raises an eyebrow. "I should look into that some time. What does he buy? Expensive ready meals covered in plastic, no doubt. Full of e-numbers."

"Don't go sticking your nose into everything, Denise," says Rita, but her voice sounds small.

I go into the kitchen to make these cups of tea. The daughter follows. She smells of perfume and cigarettes. She says she's been working abroad and now that she's back she doesn't think it's necessary for me to come every day. "Perhaps just a couple of hours a week," she says. "To clean."

I feel a hot wave of rage, but I remember to push it back down. "Mrs. Barker's son is the person who employs me," I say. "I will wait to hear from him."

"Fine," says the woman. "I'll get him to call you."

"YOU CAN'T MOVE IN HERE, DENISE," Rita shouts from the other room. "I won't HAVE it!"

Denise doesn't seem to care that I hear this. I am of no account. She is looking through the cupboards, touching the glassware and crockery. I can see her calculating her inheritance.

"These cut-glass tumblers shouldn't go in the dishwasher, Ann," she says. "In fact, they're far too valuable for daily use. Once you've made the tea perhaps you can move them to the hall cupboard. I'll show you which shelf." I can hear her scolding her mother when she goes back to the sitting room. "I see things have been allowed to slip while I've been away. What was wrong with the agency I found for you? I thought they were excellent."

Later that evening, Craig rings me. He tells me that he's just spoken to his mother. Then there is silence. Far away, on the other side of the world, he seems to be struggling with some great difficulty. I say nothing. I don't see why I should help him get rid of me.

But I'm wrong. That's not why he's called. With a lot of stammering and throat clearing, he tells me that his mother has decided she can no longer manage on her own. "I don't know your domestic situation, Ann, but my mother… well, she seems to have taken to you. She would like you to be her live-in carer." Then he names what seems to me to be an unbelievable amount of money, although later my friend tells me it should be more.

I want to say yes right away, but I know I need to talk to my friend. "I need to check some things first," I say.

"I will call you tomorrow," he says. "Thank you, Ann."

*   *   *

The next morning, I get up early and travel to the neighbourhood where I used to live with the Fisher family, to the school where I used to take the middle child every day. I stand on the opposite side of the road watching the stream of little ones until I see my children, the ones I used to care for. The middle boy has grown, but it's the youngest that takes the whole of my attention. I can't see him clearly because of his coat, but I see enough to know that he's turning into a fine child. I long for him to notice me. I want to wave and see his face light up, hear his voice call out my own true name so that I can run across the road and take him in my arms. But I control myself. It wouldn't be fair. There'd be no time to explain why I had to leave. He'd be upset. He has a whole day of school ahead of him.

They go into the playground together with a girl I've never seen before. I wait for the bell. After a minute or so this girl comes out again so I cross the road and start to walk beside her.

I tell her that I saw her come in with the Fisher boys. "Are you their new nanny?"

She tugs a set of headphones out of her ears. "Excuse me?" She has one of those open faces that belong to people who've not (yet) had any trouble in their lives. I repeat my question and she tells me everything. She is in her first year of studying geography at university. Her family is too far away for her to live at home, so she rents a room from the Fishers, which she gets a bit cheaper in exchange for taking the children to school in the mornings. In the afternoons the boys go to the after-school club and the mother or the father collects them at six. "I can't do the pickup because I have a waitressing job in the evenings. Oh! I'm so tired all the time. London is so expensive. SO expensive. I don't know how anyone manages to live here."

"Didn't they have a nanny before?" I ask. "What happened to her?"

The girl frowns, searching her memory. They did tell her the story, she says. "I think she stole something valuable. A phone, maybe? A piece of jewellery?"

I stop walking and close my eyes. I vaguely hear the girl saying she can see her bus and, "See you tomorrow!" but I don't reply. My voice doesn't work and there is the great hole in my chest where my heart used to be. I know I will never see my boy again. He is lost to me now.

* * *

When I get to Rita's, there is no sign of the daughter. I wait for Rita to ask me to be her live-in carer. Nothing. First, she wants the window open, then she wants it closed. She complains that the tea I bring her is cold and the lunch is too hot. I want to throw her plate against the wall, but I have learned what happens when you are alone among strangers and you show your true feelings. Only the rich have that luxury.

We go through the whole of my four hours until finally, just as I am getting ready to leave, she says, "So are you moving in or not?"

I sit down near her on the sofa. "Is that what you want?"

Rita shrugs her shoulders. She is so stubborn. She can't bear to have to ask for this.

I tell her that I have other work, which isn't true but she doesn't know that. "What if I give up all my other jobs and I move here, Mrs. Barker, and then your daughter tells me to go, what then?"

Rita gives me a sharp glance. "My son is the one who decides."

I don't reply.

"He said he spoke to you yesterday and you needed time to think. Well? You've had time. What do you say?"

Still, I don't speak.

"I'll tell him to offer you more money," she says.

I nod. I name the sum my friend said I should ask for. And Rita laughs, thin shoulders heaving. "Not such a doormat after all, eh! Hah! I like that."

As I leave, she yells, "Call me Rita!" as if this is a great treat for me.

This time, I tell myself, it will be easier. This time I will defend myself better. They will not get my heart.

*   *   *

The heatwave passes. The trees lose their leaves and then we're into winter. In Rita's flat it's hard to notice the difference between seasons because she likes the heating turned up high, but I have a break in the afternoons and I try to go for a walk as often as I can. I pay attention to the changes: the calm days, the stormy ones. This is my life passing. But I'm able to send money to my parents again, and to my sister and her family, and perhaps her oldest girl will be able to go to university. That is something.

In the evenings, Rita likes me to watch television with her. She enjoys darts, snooker and Formula One racing, programs that remind her of the years when she and her husband used to run a pub. His name was Alf, she tells me. He was clever as a snake. He worked out how to cheat the brewery so he could save. Then he put that money into the stock market and turned it into more, which meant they were able to buy this flat and send both children to private schools. "More fool us," she says. "Look how they turned out."

"They're making money, aren't they?"

Rita clacks her false teeth. "Money's not the only thing in life, Ann."

I don't want to start an argument so I say nothing.

Alf died of a stroke, she tells me. He was only fifty-six. "But that was a long time ago," she says. "And he had a shocking temper." About Denise she says, "We won't see her for a good while now. She's got herself another fancy job overseas. Tax free salary, company car, blah blah, all that. It won't last. There's always some bust-up and then she's back meddling in my affairs again."

I think of my parents who live near my sister so that she can look after them for nothing. Is that a good or a bad thing? I don't know any more, I only know that the world is divided into those who, like Rita's children, can buy other people's time and those—like me and the geography student—who must sell.

*   *   *

It's not even six months before Denise is back again, still smelling of tobacco and perfume, perhaps a little heavier than before, a little redder in the face.

We are watching a tense moment in the darts grand slam and Rita is not pleased to be interrupted. "What happened? Fired again?"

Denise stands for a moment watching as the challenger attempts a nine-darter. He leans forwards and Rita and I hold our breath. He's the player Rita is backing. We've started taking bets, dropping buttons in two jars beside the TV. The inset picture shows how the dart finds its target with that satisfying clunk.

"WOWZA!!!" Rita shouts. "That's my boy!"

I get up and drop another button in the *Rita* jar. "You win again, Mrs. Barker," I say. It's always a good day when Rita wins. But now, Denise picks up the remote and snaps off the TV.

"Ann, perhaps you could go for a walk? I'd like some time alone with my mother."

Rita's eyes are still on the screen. "No need to barge in like this, Denise. Whatever you want to say, you can say in front of—"

Denise fixes me with a look. "Ann? If you don't mind."

"I will be in my room."

After about half an hour, Denise comes to find me, frowning, mouth turning down at the corners. She says she's shocked by her mother's decline. "Horrified!"

I try to gather up some of my old anger to defend myself. I want to tell her that Rita has gained a little weight since I moved in; that she is always clean; that I trim her nails and cut her hair; that I massage her skin with cream to stop it cracking; that we've been doing sudoku in the morning after breakfast and she's brilliant at calculating the score in darts. I reach deep into myself looking for the energy of rage, but I've gone soft these past months.

"Thank goodness I'm back in London, that's all I can say," Denise says as she leaves. "There are going to be some changes around here, I can promise you that."

*   *   *

Denise organises an endless circus of people to come to the flat: doctors, nurses, paramedics, psychiatrists. They ask Rita to write her name and to tell them when she was born. They get her to draw a clock face and put the hands at twelve noon. They take blood. They ask if she is getting more forgetful? Does she struggle to remember names? Has she ever got lost in the flat?

"Nope," says Rita, clacking her dentures like crocodile.

We all know what Denise is up to.

"Don't worry," Rita tells me. "Craig won't let her put me in a home. He knows it would kill me."

I'm not so confident. Craig seems weak to me, and Denise is as strong as a lion. I call my brother and sister and tell them my parents must save as much as they can from the money I send. I don't know how much longer this job will last.

After a couple of weeks, Denise comes in and almost before she has taken off her coat she starts shouting about safety. "You're not SAFE, here, Mother!!! The situation is INTOLERABLE! I refuse

to have you on my conscience! I lie awake at night worrying—"
Whitish spittle is collecting in the corners of her mouth. Her color
is high. I wonder if she's a dehydrated.

"What's the trouble?" Rita says calmly. "Hotel bill due? Maxed
out your credit card?"

Denise's nicely powdered face twists into an ugly shape. "How
dare you, Mother! I'm concerned for your WELFARE!!" On and
on she goes. I can see a blue vein pulsing at her temple.

"Please, Miss Barker," I say. "Your mother is an elderly person.
Noise is not good for her. Would you like a glass of water?"

"NOISE!!!" She is shouting into my face. "How DARE YOU!
My own mother! You've no right—"

And then she goes quiet. A wave seems to pass through her body.
Her mouth falls open. Her eyes roll back in her head. I reach her
just in time to stop her hitting her head on the drinks cabinet. I
lower her to the carpet, put her in the recovery position, reach
for the phone.

From the other side of the room, I hear Rita's voice: "Just like
her father."

*   *   *

From the windows of Rita's flat we watch the spring arrive, creeping
from one tree to the next, like a slow flood of brightness. There
are daffodils in the window boxes of the flats across the street.
When I cook, I keep the kitchen window open so that I can hear
the chatter of songbirds arriving from the south. How many more
springs will Rita see? I try not to worry about that.

We watch a lot of snooker. We're still making bets. When the
Rita or the *Ann* jar of buttons is full to the top, we have a small
sherry. "Cheers," we say, "Bottoms up!", "Here's mud in your eye!"
—all these little sayings that Rita has been teaching me.

Sometimes Denise calls out to me from her room. She has
carers who visit four times a day, but I've told Craig I don't mind
helping in between. Even if she can't talk so well anymore, she's
learning ways to show me what she wants: a glass of water, her

nose or mouth wiped, sometimes a trip to the toilet. It's nothing to feel ashamed about, I tell her. We all have bodies.

At one o'clock and seven o'clock, I wheel Denise to the kitchen and the three of us eat together, and on Sundays Craig rings to ask us how things are. He is growing more confident. He makes jokes. He teases. "How are my girls?" he'll say. Once that would have put me in a rage. But I just smile and say, "We are good thank you, Craig." My friend's daughter has shown me how to set up a company for them to pay into, so I get all the money every month. They can call me whatever they like.

Rita and I get along well now. We laugh a lot. Sometimes I think about telling her the truth. I imagine myself saying: "Ann? What are you talking about? There is no Ann. My real name is—!"

But I know it would be like a firecracker in the mouth: five seconds of entertainment, then no more teeth. I can never allow myself to forget that I am the horse and they are the riders, even Denise who cannot walk anymore. So I keep my own true name to myself, something they cannot buy, something that belongs to me alone.

VICKY GRUT's *debut collection,* Live Show, Drink Included *was published by Holland Park Press and short-listed for the Edge Hill University Short Story Prize in 2019. Individual stories appeared in the* Harvard Review *and* Best British Short Stories, *2019. She lives in London.* www.vickygrut.com | @vickygrut.bsky.social

Blades of a Feather

Laura Price Steele

You're sitting at the kitchen table when the bird hits the window. See yourself there, propped up on your knees so you can reach your bowl. Feel the cereal mashed between your molars, the rough scars of the spoon—caught too many times in the spinning blade of the garbage disposal—drag against the inside of your lip.

You feel the sound at the base of your throat. The sharp *thwack*. You jolt and then freeze as if your stillness can erase what's happened. Even before you look, you know there is a body.

It's a small bird. Brown-breasted. The size of a fist. Its wings are tucked close to its body without lying all the way flat. This looks much worse than death—the bird's body lacks the soft tensionless quality of a corpse. Instead its feet are curled, its legs stiff, its skeleton somehow pulled too taut.

You slide open the door. Maybe the bird's glassy black eye follows you, but maybe not. Its beak is sharp, closed, its head turned to the side. The feathers around its neck are slightly puffed.

You know you should not touch it. Birds carry disease. Plus it is a wild thing. You know there is danger, but you can feel the inevitability in your fingertips. You still believe in magic.

The bird's belly feels like an underinflated balloon. You touch it with the back of your hand first, as if it might burn you. Its stillness feels like permission so you slide your fingers up to the soft cave under its wing. Feel the fragile bones give under the weight of your hand.

That's when the bird slips inside you.

As it happens your brain is wondering, *how? how? how?* But your body understands right away. A ghost has found its way in. Feel the drag of its feathers on the underside of your skin, feel the beak slice through the soft meat of your organs. Then the tap and settle, tap and settle as the bird makes its home behind your heart.

*   *   *

Three days after the bird hits the window, you drop into the sweaty petals of a fever. Still you can feel the bird inside of you, the lump of its body wedged into the folds of your chest.

You're sure the illness is part of the haunting. The ghost trying to smoke you out of your own body. You stay home from school and fall asleep in your clothes. When you wake, your pillow smells like boiled meat. Your parents trade off staying home to heat cans of soup on the stovetop. They press their hands to your face to test your temperature. You want to ask them not to pull away, to stand there for a while with their palm flush against your forehead, but you don't.

You can't tell your parents about the bird. They wouldn't believe you. You wouldn't believe it either, except that you never stop feeling it—the twitch and bob of its head, the opening and closing of its claws as it adjusts its grip around your ribs.

The TV murmurs. Your fever spikes. You think you might die. If you do, no one will know what killed you. You wonder if the bird will die too, or if it will be able to carve its way out of your body.

The bird stretches out its wings. Feel the hinge of its hollow bones. Feel the point of its beak reach up, up, up to the base of your throat, and dig into the flesh. It feels like your mouth will collapse into itself. The bird is asking for your silence, demanding it. You understand now—if you do not name the bird, it will let you live. You agree. You don't have to say it aloud, only think it. Silence.

By midnight, the fever breaks.

*   *   *

When you return to school, you get that small burst of celebrity from your absence. You've been out for three days. Worksheets have piled up on your desk. Kids gather around you as if you have something they might want, but the attention fades quickly.

Someone else is absent today—their chair still upside down on the desk, its legs sticking up into the air like a spider trapped on its back.

You look around the room, watch the other kids dig into their backpacks, hunch over their papers. Someone shoves a pencil into the electric pencil sharpener. The motor whirs and the sound startles you. Inside you the bird jolts, tipping forward as if readying to launch into flight. Your whole body tenses. You've heard the sound a half dozen times a day since the start of the school year, but now for the first time you hear the blade spinning, you hear the violence as the pencil sinks deeper and deeper, narrowing until its tip could draw blood.

When finally the noise stops, you look down to find that you've crumpled the edge of your paper in your fist.

*   *   *

You're sure that the bird will leave. It cannot stay in the cramped cavity of your chest. During recess you run across the dead grass between the playground and gravel. Listen to the rhythmic squeals of swing set's metal chains, a ball thwacking against the asphalt, the dull thud of feet landing in the sand.

When you reach the edge of the grass, you don't touch the light pole by the fence. Everyone knows not to. You've made the mistake before—leaned against it, felt the tiny shards of fiberglass lodge themselves in your skin. Your arm stayed red and inflamed for days, little flecks of blood working up to the surface. It didn't occur to you to mention the rash to your parents, to ask for some relief. *What were you doing rubbing against a light pole?* they would ask. Instead you wore long sleeves and waited for the evidence of your thoughtlessness to heal.

*   *   *

In the afternoon you walk home alone. The bird preens. You can feel the gentle rustle of its head as it digs its beak into its own feathers.

You walk the same route as always, along the tall fence near the school. You pass by the slope in the yard where the grass turns wild at the back, cut along the footpath near the creek. Everything is the same—the breeze coming through the trees, the chemical smell of the water, the sudsy bubbles that gather in the reeds. But now the bird is here and that gives each sensation a new weight.

Sometimes in the summer you come out here, tie a piece of lunch meat to the end of a stick, and fish for crawdads. You watch their alien bodies drift up from the murk and reach out their claws. That's the moment you love—just before you can feel the tug at the end of the stick. When they are not yet yours, but you know they will be. One time you put the crawdads in a plastic bucket and carried them home. But when you showed your parents, your dad clicked his tongue and said it was a cruel thing to do, to trap them like that. Now when you catch them, you put them in the bucket, but you don't take them home. You just watch them claw at the sides for a while as they reach up toward the sky, then you dump them back into the water.

*   *   *

When you get home, you lay on your bedroom floor. You rock your body back and forth and the bird sways inside of you, bracing itself against your momentum. It's like a piece of ice bobbing in a glass of water. That gives you an idea. You go to the kitchen sink and fill up a glass. You chug the whole thing, fill it up again. Maybe you can drown the bird.

You drink until your belly is round and distended, until you cannot feel the bird at all. You feel only the heaviness of the water, the pressure against your lungs, at the base of your throat. While you watch TV, you imagine a lake inside of your body; you see the bird floating, dead, its feathers waterlogged.

Feel the stitch of hope as you hurry to the bathroom. Listen to the angry hiss of pee and think *maybe, maybe, maybe.* You don't look into the toilet. You flush, picture the bird swirling down, down, down to nothing.

You're eating dinner when you feel the bird flick its head. You have to work to keep your face neutral, to hide the way the heat drains from your cheeks. Maybe your parents notice the way you go quiet, but they don't say anything.

All through dinner the bird shakes and shakes inside of you, like a dog that can't get itself dry. Feel the blades of its feathers fan out each time, the tips slicing into the soft meat of your insides.

*   *   *

Every afternoon before your parents get home from work, you come up with a new tactic. You hold your breath until it feels like your lungs will burst. You hang upside down from the bed. You sit in front of a bowl of milk with your mouth open. You close yourself in the basement bathroom and you flip the lights off and on, watching your pupils dilate in the mirror. You spend ten minutes lying so still you're barely even breathing, then you leap up and sprint across the yard. You eat so much ice your throat goes numb. You punch yourself in the chest. You put on your winter parka and do jumping jacks until the sweat pours down your face. You stand over a boiling pot of water with a towel over your head. You press the tip of a knife into the skin over your heart.

Nothing works. You go to bed every night feeling that fist of its body like a rock wedged under your sternum.

*   *   *

You don't tell any of your friends about the bird. But they smell it on you. They hold their bodies different than they used to, as if they might need to defend themselves against you. Conversations with them become stilted and strained. You lose the natural back-and-forth rhythm. You smile on the wrong beats. You forget to listen because you're too busy trying to come up with your next line. Sometimes you stumble into a prickly silence and you're not sure how to get out of it.

Your parents aren't suspicious. They believe it's natural for you to forget how to talk to people as you edge closer to being a teenager. Sometimes you catch them rolling their eyes at each other. Inside you the bird pecks and dips, unfolds and refolds its wings.

*   *   *

You're invited to a sleepover at a friend's house. A half dozen girls. Someone pulls out a Ouija board and you take turns pretending to let a spirit guide your hands. Maybe this is the night you'll tell someone. You can turn it into a ghost story. You can pretend the haunting does not belong to you.

But then, while you're watching someone's hands slide around the board, a girl named Liza slides up to you.

"Are you boy crazy?" she asks, grinning.

"No," you say.

"Let me test," she says and reaches over and squeezes your thigh. When her fingertips dig into your flesh, your hands automatically reach for something to swat her away. You grab your overnight bag and swing it toward her. You mean it to come off playfully. But you forget that this is the bag you take to the public pool, that there's a padlock at the bottom of it.

You can feel the sound in your jaw—the crack of Liza's skull. And then blood is pouring out of her forehead and the other girls are screaming. "Oh my god, oh my god." You want everyone to pause so you can explain yourself. But the girls are grabbing towels, holding them to Liza's face. Someone starts yelling for a parent. They move toward the stairs, the five of them like one single being. And you are separate from them.

As they stumble up the stairs, you feel the thrum of the bird's heartbeat as if it is your own.

Once Liza's in the car to the hospital, the rest of the girls call their parents to get picked up. They don't say anything to you.

They just keep telling the story to each other. "That was so crazy," they say over and over.

Right away, you know the story will stick to you forever. The way Brett B. will always be the kid who ate rocks on the playground or Gabe will always be the one who peed himself at the winter concert. You'll always be the girl who split Liza's face open at a slumber party.

You call your house, ask your dad to come get you. You don't tell him what happened. But someone calls your parents the next day and they sit you down and you have to tell them the story. When you mention the padlock at the bottom of the bag, their eyebrows go up and don't come down. You're not sure if your parents believe you when you say you forgot the lock was in there.

Your mom tells you to make a card for Liza. You think you're going to put it in the mail, but then your mom drives you over to her house. You don't even know where her house is and you don't know how your mom knows. But there you are standing on her doorstep. Liza and her mom answer the door together. Liza has a bandage on her forehead, gauze wrapped around her head to hold it in place. You feel a surge of jealousy—everyone can see the exact location of her pain.

Neither Liza nor her mom invite you in. You hold out the card. Your mom says that of course they'll pay for the trip to the ER, and Liza's mom sniffs. "She'll probably have a scar," she says.

"We are both so sorry," your mom says and she pinches your arm.

"I'm really sorry," you say and the words feel like clumps of wet tissue in your mouth.

"Thanks," Liza says, taking the card, never looking you in the face.

On the front of the card, you drew a bird, and the bird is saying *Get Well Soon*. Inside you, the bird opens its mouth like it's trying to scream.

*   *   *

When you're alone, you go back over that night again and again, feel the way your hand reached for the bag, try to suss out whether any part of you remembered the padlock. Every time you feel your arm swing, the bird pitches itself forward like it's bracing for an impact. You can't tell in the memory if the bird was readying itself for violence, if it knew the blood was coming. But the possibility needles you.

Now, even when the bird goes quiet, you never forget about it; you are always waiting for its movement. Some portion of your attention turns permanently inward. You are split in half—one part of you looking out, the other tending the bird, minding the way it rubs against the cage of your bones.

It's there all the time. Anything can remind you of the frantic hammering of its heart—the sliver of confusion when you wake; the whoosh and bump of a car door closing; the way water gathers at your lips in the shower; a stranger leaning past you to grab something off a grocery store shelf; the clatter of a dropped cell phone; the sudden blindness when the sun catches your eyelids and blots out your vision; the whisper at an assembly about the vice principal's cleavage; the way a chair dragged against the ground can sound almost like a scream; the thump of an elbow or shoulder pushing by in the hallway; the flicker of a street light; the sting of a papercut; the shock of reaching into a bag and finding some wetness you didn't expect; a walk signal flipping to the flashing orange hand; a chair tipping over and crashing onto the linoleum; two boys running into each other during PE, blood bursting from one's mouth; an unleashed dog charging at you; brakes screeching; a news story about a woman folded into a suitcase and left on the side of the highway; a glass slipping from your hands and shattering in the sink; the dark pause between a question and its answer.

Always you are reaching for the bird, feeling it before you feel anything else. The way it startles, the way its body curls, its weight sinking just barely as it readies to burst into flight.

*   *   *

Over time you and the bird become like the white and yolk of an egg. You don't exist without one another. No longer does it feel like the bird has made a home inside of you. Now it is part of what makes your body a home—the same way your tongue lays just so against your teeth or the way your hands grab for each other.

The story inverts itself. Now you reach for the bird to remind yourself that you exist. Sometimes it feels like that's the only thing keeping you tethered to your body.

You cannot remember what you felt like before the bird. Even your early memories are tinged with inevitability. The bird was always coming for you.

You think it'll go on like this forever, your body a cage. Even as you get older and you stop believing in ghosts and monsters, you never doubt the bird's existence. You never think it is anything other than what it is.

*   *   *

One night you go to a party at some house you've never been to. You're in high school now. You have a part-time job as a hostess at a restaurant. One of the busboys invited you. His name is Oscar and he is always licking his teeth.

There are too many bodies in the rooms. A steady thump of music. Feel the wild in the air. A promise of something like rage. You hate it but you crave it. The sour smells, the way people steady themselves against the walls even if they're not yet drunk. It's like being in a fun house together. The rules are gone. Gravity isn't gravity anymore.

A boy sleeps on the stairs. He has no shirt and there's a bright red mark across his back. A hole in the drywall nearby.

"Holy shit," someone says, a girl's voice. You turn and there is Liza. Your stomach drops. You haven't seen her in a few years. She moved after seventh grade. Her makeup is thick and her eyes are a little bit glassy. "It's you."

"Hey," you say.

"I still have a fucking scar," she says, but she's smiling like it's some kind of inside joke between you.

"Yeah?" You lean close to her, squint.

"Here." She grabs your hand and puts your fingertips on her forehead. It just feels like a forehead.

"I didn't know the lock was in there," you say.

"What?" she says.

"I didn't know there was a padlock at the bottom of my bag. I thought it was just an empty bag."

"Oh," she says, like you're trying to reshape her memory.

"How many stitches was it?" you ask.

"Twelve," she says, touching the middle of her forehead lightly.

"Whoa." You don't know whether that's a lot of stitches or not.

"Nothing like that had ever happened to me," she says. Her brow furrows and maybe you can see the scar.

"Me neither," you say. And she shoots you a dark look, like she's caught you in a lie.

"I'd take it back if I could," you say.

"You can't," she says. Not meanly, just matter of fact. She shrugs. "I'm going to go find a drink."

"Good to see you," you say, even though the phrase feels misshapen coming out of your mouth.

*   *   *

After that, you slip into the bathroom. The toilet is wobbly, a candle has melted onto the edge of the sink. Someone has added water to the bottle of hand soap to make it last.

That's when it happens. Just before you leave the bathroom, you look in the mirror. It's not intentional really. As you turn toward the door, you catch sight of yourself. The bird flutters. You don't say anything out loud. But for the first time you hold the words in your head. *A ghost bird lives inside of me.*

Maybe it is the unfamiliar place, the stink of it, the strange shadows cast by the single bare bulb. But for the first time you look plainly at the truth. All at once you understand the absurdity, the impossibility. There is no bird.

*   *   *

A chasm opens up inside of you. The bird is gone. Without the weight of it, something else seeps in. Feel the jagged edges of a new memory. You cannot bring it into focus yet, but it's there—the heaviness, another body trying to split you in half with a dull knife. Remember the panic in your chest, the sensation of being trapped. The sour taste of fear. There is no bird in this memory, it is only you and the damp breath of another mouth, your skin rubbed raw, the brutality of someone else's want. Feel the tender flesh of your throat, the wound between your legs.

You wonder if maybe the bird sacrificed itself to spare you from this memory. You feel a sudden tenderness toward it. Sometimes in the dark you could see it, the glassy black globes of its eyes, its long, strange claws. All this time you wanted it gone, and now it is. Vanished. But you didn't know what it was guarding against; you didn't understand that one haunting could forestall another.

Before you have time to question whether a bird ever hit the window at all, you push out of the bathroom and down the hallway. Someone stumbles by, drops a plastic cup onto the carpet. You hustle to the front door, step out into the night.

Outside, the neighborhood is quiet. You walk around the side of the house to the alley. One half of the dumpster lid is thrown open. You can smell the rich stink of the garbage, so rotten it's turned almost sweet.

The front door of the house swings open and someone steps out onto the porch. You can only see the outline of their body and the orange glow of their cigarette. Since you don't announce yourself right away, you stay quiet, let the person think they are alone. You believe it is a kindness, not spoiling their illusion.

It's hypnotizing almost, watching a stranger's breath move through the ember of their cigarette. Let yourself be entranced by it. Let the whole world narrow to that tiny orange circle.

*   *   *

You will return to this night over and over again, wear the memory thin by handling it too much. Sometimes, in the murkiness between wake and sleep, you'll remember the sensation of something solid inside you turning to ash. You'll jerk awake, legs thrashing, heart beating wild, and you'll wish the bird back to its cage.

Years from now, you'll find yourself in this part of town for some errand. You'll try to find this house again to prove it exists. But you'll get turned around, lost in the one-way streets. It won't matter. Even if you drive right by it, you won't recognize it in the daylight, when everything monstrous can look so benign.

The truth is your brain will never stop playing the cat and mouse game of what's real and what's created. But that's later. Now you are standing in the damp cold. Feel the give of weeds under your feet. Watch the cigarette arc back and forth from the invisible mouth.

The bird is gone, yes. But picture it overhead, swooping into flight. Feel its quivering body, curled inside you for so long, finally spreading out. The moonlight spilling off its feathers. See it rising, rising, rising until the city smears below it, until the only things with any borders are its body and the moon.

LAURA PRICE STEELE is a writer and editor who lives in Missoula, Montana with her wife and daughters. She has been the winner of the Ploughshares *Emerging Writer's Contest in nonfiction as well as the Montana Prize in Fiction. Her work has been published by or is forthcoming from* Ploughshares, CutBank, The Sun, *and* The Iowa Review, *among others. She earned her MFA from the University of North Carolina Wilmington.*

9 798990 183858